IN THE MIDNIGHT HOWL

Peculiar Mysteries & Romances

RENEE GEORGE

Barkside of the Moon Press

In The Midnight Howl

Peculiar Mysteries Book 5

Copyright © Renee George 2017

Cover Art: Renee George

Print September 4, 2017

ISBN-10: 1947177044

ISBN-13: 978-1947177048

PARANORMAL MYSTERIES & ROMANCES

By Renee George

Peculiar Mysteries & Romances

Nora Black Midlife Psychic Mysteries

Age of Inno-Scents (Book 6)
Aroma Holiday (Book 7)

Witchin' Impossible Paranormal Mysteries

Witchin' Impossible (Book 1)
Rogue Coven (Book 2)
Familiar Protocol (Booke 3)
Mr & Mrs. Shift (Book 4)

Barkside of the Moon Paranormal Mysteries

Pit Perfect Murder (Book 1)
Murder & The Money Pit (Book 2)
The Pit List Murders (Book 3)
Pit & Miss Murder (Book 4)
The Prune Pit Murder (Book 5)
Two Pits and A Little Murder (Book 6)
Pits and Pieces of Murder (Book 7)

Grimoires of a Middle-aged Witch

Earth Spells Are Easy (Book 1)
Spell On Fire (Book 2)
When the Spells Blows (Book 3)
Spell Over Troubled Water (Book 4)
Ghost in the Spell (Book 5)

Hex Drive

Hex Me, Baby, One More Time (Book 1)
Oops, I Hexed It Again (Book 2)
I Want Your Hex (Book 3)
Hex Me With Your Best Shot (Book 4)

Hex Me All Night Long (Book 5)

Madder Than Hell
Gone With The Minion (Book 1)
Devil On A Hot Tin Roof (Book 2)
A Street Car Named Demonic (Book 3)

ACKNOWLEDGMENTS

This book was a muse and coffee-fueled driven piece of love. Willy and Brady's story was so special and lovely to write. I especially loved getting to know Ruth better. She and Willy make the best BFFs. And on that note, I have some very special people in my own life that I must acknowledge and thank.

For Robbin, thank you for pushing me and staying up with me and brainstorming the shit out of this book with me. I should be kissing your ass every day. For Jeanna, you are the queen of continuity!! Thank you for jumping on board as a proofer and reader, I love you!! And lastly, but not leastly, (all of these ladies are first in my book!) Michele Bardsley for all her great edits, suggestions, and revisions. You are my QUEEN!

Next, I have to thank my Rebel Readers. I ADORE you guys! Thank you for being loyal fans. XXXOOOXXXOOO. I also want to thank the Peculiar Fans for making this mystery romance series one of my best sellers! I will keep writing them as long as you want to keep reading them.

I also want to thank the town of Peculiar, whose name I borrowed then used my creative fiction license to relocated them from the north of Missouri to down south in the Ozarks, for giving me a kick ass place to start. Stay peculiar, Peculiar!

BLURB

Intrigue, murder, and a town full of suspects will test Wilhelmina "Willy" Boden's investigative skills as an outsider in Peculiar.

*****

When an anonymous whistleblower from Peculiar, Missouri alleges that the mayor's wife is a fraud, the Shifter Tri-State Council decides to send me in to investigate. Problem is, I like the people in this town, and I don't want to betray any of them...especially a certain handsome were-coyote named Brady Corman.

Unfortunately, I don't get paid to make friends or dates.

But when the local pain-in-the-ass aka "the whistle-blower" is found dead, and both the town's beloved Sheriff and Brady's teenaged son are prime suspects, along with half the town, I have to investigate.

As much as I'd like to ignore the evidence, my sense of

duty won't let me turn a blind eye to injustice. My loyalty to my friends will be tested and my relationship with Brady may be over before it even begins.

What's a werebobcat to do when my instincts tell her one thing and my heart the exact opposite?

For Simon.
You came into my life when I
didn't want another cat and
you made me yours.

CHAPTER ONE

*F*or more than a year, I had dreamed, no, fantasized about getting back to Peculiar, Missouri. My first visit last June during the Tri-State Council Jubilee had made me fall in love with the town. I'd made friends. Sunny Haddock, who was married to the mayor Babel Trimmel, was funny, sweet and self-deprecating. I could hang out with her all day doing nothing and still have a blast. Chavvah Trimmel, Sunny's best friend and sister-in-law, not to mention all around bad-ass chick, was one of the most solid people I'd ever met. But I think I liked Ruth Thompson the best.

Ruth was the kind of woman, whom on paper, I would never have imagined as a friend. She'd been married more than twenty years, had nine kids, and seemed to know the dirt on everyone in the small community. And last, but certainly not least, on that list of awesome people was sexy, broody Brady Corman. We'd had a moment when I'd been in Peculiar for Halloween, and I'd hoped to take that sizzling connection and turn it into an extended adventure.

But right now, as I avoided the gazes of those people I'd wanted to call friends, I knew whatever chance I'd had to be a part of Peculiar—and part of Brady's life—was gone. As an investigator for the Council, I had a job to do, and I took my oath and duty very seriously. That's why I was here, at this moment, destroying my new friendships.

I turned to Sheriff Taylor and said, "I'm sorry, Sid, you know I don't want to do this."

"It's okay, Willy."

"I have to make it official."

He nodded. "I understand."

"Sheriff Sidney Taylor of Peculiar, Missouri, in accordance with the terms of therianthropic protocol as regulated by the Tri-State Council, I have the authority to relieve you of your duty in this investigation and suspend you from this office until said investigation is resolved." This last part killed me to say. "I'll need your badge and weapon."

Sheriff Taylor, his eyes unnaturally dark, which was saying a lot since he's a raccoon shifter, took his badge from his shirt and placed it on Deputy Farraday's desk. Next, he unholstered his gun and set it down next to the silver star. His gaze scraped across the office at his people, including Deputies Farraday, Connelly, and Thompson. Mayor Babel Trimmel, Sunny, Chavvah, Dr. Smith, Ruth Thompson, the sheriff's wife, Jean, and their daughter, Nicole. There was a rise of protest throughout the group, but Sheriff Taylor raised his hand.

"I stand by what I did," he said, his voice as tired as his eyes. He looked at his daughter. "I'd do it again."

"Dad," she said.

Sheriff Taylor held his head high, stoic in his resignation. "Don't."

"Oh, Sid," Jean said and threw her arms around him. She turned an accusing finger at me. "He trusted you. How could you do this?"

In the face of all the disappointed and angry glares from the gathered crowd, I wanted to relent, tell everyone what a big mistake I made. However, he had hidden evidence in a crucial investigation. His choice. Which is why the Council had pulled rank and forced me into this despicable situation.

FOUR DAYS EARLIER...

"You're here!" Ruth said, standing in the open doorway to her two-story pink house with blue trim. "I've made up Dakota's room for you. She'll be sharing a bed with Michele while you're here."

Yellow and purple flowers lined the concrete walkway leading to her front porch, painting a real pretty picture of rural living. "I don't want to put you through any trouble," I told the enthusiastic deer shifter. "I could have just stayed in the motel."

"Oh, pish-posh. I'll hear none of that. Ed, the kids, and I are happy to have you. Besides, I've baked three pies for your visit, so you have to--"

3

I waved my hand. "You had me at pie."

Ruth laughed. "Good. Now, let's get your bags inside." I only had one suitcase and a vanity. "I'm so excited to see you again. I'm glad you decided to come down for your vacation."

"I needed a little getaway from the old job," I lied. The fib, and not a little white one, made me feel like shit. I did not want to keep things from Ruth. But telling the truth, in this case, would be so much worse. The Tri-State Council had sent me to Peculiar to investigate a rumor about Sunshine "Sunny" Trimmel. They'd received an anonymous letter from a whistleblower that stated, "The mayor's wife isn't what you think she is. Sunny Trimmel is an imposter." Personally, I didn't care whether Sunny was a marshmallow creature from the moon, she'd become a friend, and I didn't particularly like spying on people I cared about.

Better me than someone else though. At least I would operate under the impression that Sunny was innocent until proven guilty, unlike some of my jackass counterparts. The Tri-State Council had officially praised Peculiar and its police force for solving a several-years-old murder spree. Never the less, the killers had been the president of the Tri-State Council's sons, and while it wasn't Chavvah or Sunny's fault, there had been some misdirected hard feelings toward the pair of friends.

Ruth insisted on taking the larger suitcase, and after the long drive down, I didn't have the energy to argue. Besides, I don't think I'd have won if I'd tried.

I loved Ruth's home. Especially the kitchen. It held a

genuine warmth, a feeling of family. I followed her through the living room to a narrow stairwell, and we traveled up to the second floor.

"Dakota's room is just up on the left here. The door at the end of the hall is the bathroom. What time do you normally get up in the morning?"

"Usually around seven. Why?"

"I'll make sure the kids stay out of there from seven to seven-fifteen." She smiled. "With nine people in the house, even with three bathrooms, one on the second floor, two downstairs, we have to use a system or chaos reigns."

I laughed. "I can see that."

"Here we are," Ruth said brightly. She opened the door.

Her oldest daughter's room was painted a soft rose with a darker pink border decorated in pastel blue swooshes around the ceiling. Her queen-sized bed was covered in a buttercream quilted comforter with royal blue and buttercream throw pillows stacked by the headboard. There was typical fare like pictures of her and her friends attached to a memory board, band posters, and various mementos. The furniture consisted of a rustic white-washed dresser, a matching bedside stand, a vanity with a lighted mirror, and a chair with the seat covered in the same royal blue as the pillows. On the stand, was a lamp with a pink lampshade and a dog-eared copy of Michele Bardsley's *I'm The Vampire, That's Why*. I was a fan of the Broken Heart Vampires, so I approved.

"You in the mood for a little outing?" Ruth said as we hauled my bags into the room.

"What you got in mind?"

5

"Michele is doing community theater." Ruth's pert nose wrinkled in a way that told me she was hiding something. "I'd like to watch the rehearsal."

"Uhm, sure." I gave her some direct eye contact. "Is there something else?"

"Well..." A small smile tugged at the corners of her lips. "I thought it'd be fun."

"And?"

"And, you know... Oh! Sunny's directing. You'd like to see Sunny, right? You haven't been back since Halloween."

I did want to see Sunny, even with the guilt poking at my gut. "What else?" She was keeping something back.

Ruth scratched her head behind her ear and wiggled her mouth. Finally, after a super heavy sigh, she confessed, "Brady is set building today. I thought you might want to say hello. I mean, you all seemed to get along so well at the Halloween party."

Ugh. The Halloween fiasco. The Johnson's barn went up in flames, and it almost ended in disaster for Brady's son Jo Jo. But that wasn't the fiasco I meant. I'd thought Brady was handsome the first time I saw him last June. A little broken, but that had made him even more irresistible to me. I had a history of picking unavailable or emotionally damaged men. Brady, it turned out, had been a little of both. We'd had a real moment that evening. A connection. Until I kissed him, and he ran off like his tail was on fire.

"I don't think anything will be happening between Brady Corman and myself."

"Well, then don't come for Brady. Come for Sunny. Come for me. I'd love the company."

"As long as you don't play matchmaker."

Ruth grinned. "Deal."

THE COMMUNITY CENTER was down on Riverfront Street. It was only five small town blocks from Ruth's house, so we walked. Damn, I loved this town. The sky seemed bluer in Peculiar. The grass greener, the trees lusher, and the air sweeter. I envied the folks who lived here year-round. I lived on the Kansas side of Kansas City in a busy, hectic, noisy neighborhood. It was a short drive to the Tri-State Council offices in Overland Park, which made it convenient for work, but I'd never thought about how much I hated apartment living until I'd spent time in this little town. Now, Peculiar was all I could think about.

"Laertes, you're up," I heard Sunny say with some authority. "Take it from act one, scene two. Claudius says, What would'st thou have, Laertes?"

Eight men and three women crowded the small stage. One of the women, I recognized as Ruth's daughter Michele, one was a plain jane with dark curly hair, and the third, who sat on a crafted throne, had black hair pulled back in a severe bun.

Eldin Farraday, a deputy with the Peculiar Sheriff's Department, stumbled out on stage. His cheeks flushed. "Sorry. Sorry," he said.

The black-haired woman's face pinched with irritation. "This is ridiculous." She stood up and straightened her skirt. "How are we supposed to put on a proper play when half the cast doesn't take it seriously?"

"I take my part plenty serious," Eldin said.

From the back of the community theater, a spotlight pinpointed the woman's face. She threw up her hand to block the blinding light. "What in the blazes?" she exclaimed.

The spotlight went out. I looked back to see Taylor Thompson, one of Ruth's twins, wave his hand. "Sorry. My bad." There was a twinkle of mischief in his eyes.

I liked that young man. I turned back to the stage to study the irritated woman. She reminded me of some of the women who used to flutter around my dad when I was young. He was a leader in our community. Without a mate, he'd become a prime candidate for the vultures who wanted to be his wife for the status alone. They were the kind of creatures who yearned for power, if only on a small scale, and were only happy if everyone else was afraid. This woman worked at breeding fear.

"Now, Evelyn," Sunny said. "We'll get all the kinks worked out before opening night. You just let me worry about the details."

"I'll thank you to mind who you're talking to," Evelyn snapped. "I'm not going to take sass from a--"

"Hello," Ruth shouted. "Look who I have with me!"

Sunny's eyes widened with pleased surprise when she saw me. "Willy!" Her hair was longer and blonder—and hey, she wasn't pregnant for once. She bounded down the aisle to me and clasped me by the shoulders before dragging me into a spine crunching hug.

"Hey, girl." I squeezed her back. Guilt pinched at me, and I brushed it aside. "It's so good to see you." I leaned back to get a better look at her. No bags or dark circles under her eyes. Her figure was back to pre-pregnancy shape, and, for a mom of two babies, she appeared remarkably well-rested. "You look great."

"Thanks," she said. "I feel great. What are you doing back in town? Can't get enough of Peculiar night life?"

I chuckled and hoped it didn't sound as forced as it felt. I nodded toward the stage. "Who's the bitch?"

Sunny didn't even turn around to see who I was looking at. "Evelyn Meyers. The town's conscience."

Ruth snorted. "That's one word for it. I can't believe she and Jean Taylor are sisters. Jean is such a lovely woman.'"

Jean was Sheriff Taylor's wife. I'd gotten to know them on my first trip to Peculiar. I'd even had dinner at their home. Watching Evelyn now, I could see the familial resemblance. "I'd fire her cranky ass," I said.

"I can't," Sunny said. Under her breath, she added, "She's funding the whole thing."

Ruth moved in closer and said in a hushed voice, "How's Michele doing?"

"Why are we whispering?"

"Because I don't want her to think I'm checking up on her."

"But you are," I pointed out.

Sunny giggled. "Michele is killing it as Ophelia," Sunny gushed.

Ruth beamed with pride.

Sunny looked at me, her face going curiously blank for about three seconds. When she animated again, she said, "Brady is backstage building the graveyard set. You should go back and see him."

I gave a quick shake of my head. "Nah. I'm sure I'll see him later." Or maybe not. I mean, I wanted to see him, but I liked myself too much to put myself in a position to get shot down again.

"That's not the line, you ignorant child," Evelyn screeched from the stage. Her well-timed tirade took the Brady heat off me for the moment. I looked past Sunny to see who was getting the brunt of her ire.

Jo Jo stood in front of Evelyn, fists clenched, his face red with anger and embarrassment. "It is the line, Ms. Meyers." He held up his copy of the play. "Unless William Shakespeare wrote more than one version."

Evelyn blanched. "You're fired, Jolon Corman. Fired!"

Jo Jo tossed his script down and stormed off the stage. He stopped when he got to Sunny. "Someday someone is going to put that witch in her place."

"Don't go," Sunny said. "I'll take care of this."

"I can't deal with her today." He shook his head. "I'll go see if Chav needs help with the new guy at the cafe." When Sunny wasn't a play director, mother of two, and wife to the mayor, she ran the vegetarian café she co-owned with Chavvah. Yeah, I know. A vegetarian café in a shifter town was weird, but for Peculiar it worked.

"You'll come back though, Jo Jo? This play needs its Hamlet."

He glared up at the stage, his green eyes flashing with

animosity. "Yeah, I'll be back." He looked at Sunny. "But for you, not for her."

After he had left, Sunny sashayed down the aisle, a bright smile on her face. "You can't fire Jo Jo," she told the older woman.

"Should we go help?" I asked.

Ruth shook her head. "Sunny can handle Evelyn."

"I'm paying for this play." Meyers stood up and crossed her arms. "I can fire who I want."

Sunny's whole body stilled. She walked up the four steps to the stage. With her hands on her hips, she smiled even bigger at Evelyn who had sat back down on her makeshift throne. "While it might be difficult, I'm certain I can find someone else to play Queen Gertrude if your choice is to pull your money and leave." She looked over her shoulder. "Hey, Ruth, how do you feel about Shakespeare?"

"Jo Jo can stay," interrupted Evelyn. She sniffed. "So long as he gets his lines right from now on."

Sunny's smile turned nearly feral. "If you get the urge to fire anyone else, Evelyn, you'll be doing this play alone."

The cast on stage all nodded, silently agreeing to walk out with Sunny.

"I'm scared of her," I told Ruth. "She's fierce."

"Sunny's very good with people." Ruth wrinkled her nose. "Why do you think we asked her to be the director? She has a gift."

A gift I was sent to uncover. What had anonymous meant when they'd written, "She's not one of us." The way most of the community loved and defended Sunny, I'd say there wasn't anyone who was one of them more than the blonde wonder.

"Hey, Sunny. Do you want the gravesite on wheels or furniture slides?" a deep, rough voice asked.

It froze me in place. Brady Corman walked out from behind the curtain, all six-foot, sexy-as-hell, melt-my-panties coyote shifter. Wow. I honest to goodness swooned. I waited for him to notice me. It took all of about two seconds.

"Uhm, I'll figure it out," he told Sunny and escaped back behind the curtains.

His reaction, or lack thereof, disappointed me. "This is ridiculous."

"I'm sorry, Willy." Ruth put her hand on my shoulder. "I just thought... Oh, well. It's nothing a little sweet tea, apple pie, and some good company can't fix." She whistled up at the stage. "You all wrapping this up soon? Maybe Chavvah can take a break and join us?"

"Sure, that's probably a good idea, considering." Sunny gave Evelyn a pointed look. The woman's expression soured even more. I got the feeling Evelyn didn't like people who stood up to her. Sunny circled her finger. "Let's take a break and meet back here at four to rehearse Act One Scene Two, which means I'll need Evelyn, Milo, Roger, Michele, Eldin, and Sabrina to come back. I'll message Jo Jo, Billy Bob, and Elton. The first scene is nailed, but the second scene is a hot mess."

"Because some people don't take it seriously," Evelyn said. Sunny pivoted to glare at the woman. Evelyn shut up, even though her face still looked like she was sucking on lemons.

"When are they putting this play on?" I asked Ruth out the side of my mouth.

"In eight weeks," she whispered.

"How long have they been rehearsing?"

"Three weeks."

"I'm afraid two months isn't going to be enough time."

Ruth smiled. "Sunny will get them there."

"You have a lot of faith in her, don't you?"

"She's one of the most genuine people I know," Ruth said.

That's not what the anonymous letter had said. "How long has she been in Peculiar?"

"About two years now."

"And was she an integrator, or is she from another therian community?"

Ruth hesitated, then said, "Uhm, she lived in San Diego before here."

"So, integrator?" Integrators were therianthropes who lived in human populated areas and hid their real selves from everyone around them. Technically, I was an integrator now since going to work for the Council, but my dad had raised my brother and me in a small therian town in southern Kansas near Oklahoma.

"Sure," Ruth said a little too brightly. She blinked then lightly smacked her forehead with her palm. "Oh, shoot. I'm supposed to pick up Linus from his summer camp. I don't know what's going on with the boy, but he can get a little dramatic if I'm late."

I snorted. "My brother once cried because I got one more marshmallow in my bowl of cereal than he did. Believe me, I know dramatic." My younger brother Hans is needy, which is just a nice way of saying he's a big fucking baby. "You get on out of here and get him, I'll meet you over at Sunny's Outlook when you get back."

While Sunny gave last minute orders to her cast, Eldin Farraday made his way down to me. His gray-green eyes made his ordinary face memorable. He was tall, thin, and handsome, and close to my age, and to top it off, he was a really good deputy. He'd been instrumental in taking down the Lowry brothers last June. Why couldn't I fall for a guy like that? Sweet, uncomplicated, and reliable.

"Hey, Willy," Eldin said. "Nice to see you back in town."

"It's nice to be seen." I smiled. "Laertes, huh? You know he buys it in the last act."

"Now you went and ruined the whole play for me." Eldin chortled, an easy laugh, his eyes crinkling at the edges. "And here I thought I was playing the hero."

"Well, they don't call the play Laertes, do they?" I laughed. He really was a nice man. "You want to come over to Sunny's Outlook for some lunch with Sunny and me?"

A throat cleared behind me. Eldin's face brightened. Taylor Thompson, the thinner of Ruth's oldest boys, raised his brow at the deputy. I nearly got burned from the sparks arcing between the two. Well, that was that. I checked Eldin Farraday off my list of eligible bachelors.

Eldin smiled at me. "Sorry, Willy. I've got plans. Maybe another time."

"You got it," I said. As the two men walked out of the

community center, I felt a small pang of jealousy. How awesome would it be for Brady to look at me like that?

The next thing I knew Evelyn Meyers stood next to me, her arms crossed over her chest. "Those two should be ashamed." The unpleasant woman was a few inches taller than me, no big shocker. I was usually the shortest girl in a room of therians. "It's unnatural."

"Oh, c'mon," I said. "A deputy dating a civilian isn't against the law."

She gaped at me. "Are you seriously that dense?"

I took a tool from Sunny's people-skills bag and smiled widely. "Don't you find intolerance more unnatural? I'd rather be around two dudes in love than someone bitter and judgmental."

Evelyn glared at me. "I know why you're here, Ms. Boden. You'll be better served by doing your job and keeping your opinions to yourself."

Same to you, honey.

She stomped off, muttering under her breath.

Sunny joined me as I watched Evelyn go.

"That woman needs to get laid," said Sunny.

I choked on a laugh. "She needs something." One thing was certain, I might not know Sunny's secret, but Evelyn Meyers probably did. My heart sunk at the thought of that awful woman being whistleblower. I'd have to have a private chat with the wicked witch of Peculiar, and soon.

CHAPTER TWO

*A*t one in the afternoon, Sunny's Outlook was a packed house. The cowbell over the door rang out every minute like a warning bell. Chavvah Trimmel stood behind the counter. She wore her dark brown hair pulled back in a ponytail, which highlighted her high cheekbones and generous mouth. I'd read a little about her history from the report Sid Taylor had turned into the council. She'd been kidnapped and tortured for several weeks by a bunch of rich asshole humans who'd discovered our kind and decided we were big game sport. There wasn't much written up after her rescue. I imagined it had been hard to come back from something so heinous, but she not only came back, she was stronger than ever.

"Hey, Willy!" Chavvah grinned.

"Hey, Chav." I hugged her when she came around the counter. Again, the guilt. I hated that I wasn't in Peculiar for a simple vacation.

Sunny came up behind me. "Get this girl a jackfruit burger, extra jalapenos and a side of sweet potato fries."

"Wow, how did you know that's what I wanted?" I'd been craving that damn burger for months now.

Sunny tapped her temple and smiled. "Mind like a steel trap."

"More like a rusty colander," Chavvah said. "Didn't you forget that you were supposed to relieve me an hour ago so I could go meet Billy Bob at the courthouse?"

"Shoot!" Sunny's panic was palpable. "I'm so sorry. Is it too late to go now?" She was already tying her hair back. She fixed it with a blue cotton hair band. She sighed and sagged against the counter. "Don't be mad at me. I know the mayor. I can make this right."

"I know the mayor, too," Chav said crossly.

"What do you need to go to the courthouse for? Traffic ticket?"

"To speak with Mary Jane Adams about renting her wedding venue. She works part-time at the courthouse and said she'd fit us in today. Her place really books up."

My eyes widened. "Really? It's about time!" I'd been privileged to witness Billy Bob's proposal. It had been sexy and romantic. "When's the wedding date?"

"In three months, if we can get our ducks in a row."

Sunny slung on an apron and shoved Chav toward the door. "Get to quacking, missy. I got this place covered."

Chav snickered and shook her head. "I'll be back in an hour." To me, she added, "If you're going to be around later, I'd love to catch up."

"You got it."

Sunny went around to the kitchen door and called back my order. There was a line forming behind me. "I'm sorry," she said. "Just grab an empty seat if you can find one. I'll join you as soon as I can."

There were people in every booth, and two of the three tables were taken. The third, near the bathroom door, was the only one open.

Jo Jo passed me with a tray of empty dishes. "What can I get you to drink?"

"A root beer would be nice."

He winked. "You got it."

Jo Jo looked nothing like his dad. He was taller, thinner, and a lot more pierced. I counted twelve piercings on his head alone. But that charming smile, that was all Brady. "Don't get cheeky," I teased.

I swear he looked like he grew two inches as he strolled back toward the kitchen. I was still smiling when I noticed Brady sitting alone in the corner booth, just a couple feet away. He stared at me like I'd grown three noses and whistled through each of them. When our gazes met, he turned his attention to his steaming cup of black coffee. I could almost see the wheels spinning as he contemplated what to do next.

"Don't fret. I won't bother you if that's what you're worried about."

"I'm not worried," he said, meeting my gaze once again.

I forced a smile. "Liar."

A slight sheen of sweat from a day of hard work coated his brow. He had a five o'clock shadow, and his hair looked like it was three weeks overdue for a trim. He wore jeans and a white T-shirt stained with dirt and sprinkled with sawdust. Basically, he fulfilled every blue-collar fantasy I'd ever had. God, why did this man have to look so damn good?

"I'm not worried," he said again. His eyes softened, and his lopsided smile deepened the dimples in his cheeks. This was the Brady who I'd been dreaming about since October.

Jo Jo came back with my root beer. He gave his dad an odd look. "You okay? You need your coffee heated up?"

"No, I'm good." Brady cleared his throat. "You, uh, remember Ms. Boden don't you?"

"Yep." Jo Jo took his lower lip barbell between his teeth. "I know Willy. Why are you acting so weird?"

I widened my eyes. "Yeah, Brady, why are you acting so weird?"

He grunted. "I'm not."

"You should join him, Willy. I think eating alone is dulling his brain."

"Why, Jo Jo, I think you might be right." I got up and went to the booth, sliding onto the bench opposite Brady. "Hello there."

His cheeks flushed, and if I didn't know better, I'd say he looked pleased. "Hello."

"Good." Jo Jo grabbed the root beer from my table and set it in front of me. "Your food will be ready in a few minutes."

I leaned on my elbows and took a sip of my cold, sweet root beer. "What's up?"

"The usual." He took a drink of coffee. "What's up with

you?"

"Oh, you know, the usual." Since we were being so honest with each other. "Nice weather we're having."

He raised an annoyed brow. "What are you doing?"

"Small talk. I thought that's what we both were doing."

"All right," he said. "I'll play. Yes, Willy. Nice weather. The Royals played a good game against Minnesota last night."

I smiled. "They played the Mariners last night."

Brady shrugged and took another drink of coffee. "I took a stab. I knew it was something with an M. I don't really watch, but Jo Jo had the game on when I got home last night."

"Okay, you don't like sports. What do you like?"

"Short redheads with pert freckly noses, bright green eyes, and curves that would give J-Lo a run for her money," Sunny said. At our surprised expressions, she added, "It's only a guess." She put down two plates of food, the jackfruit burger plate for me and a monster cinnamon roll for Brady. "You two enjoy your food now."

"Don't mind Sunny," I said. The aroma of tangy sweet barbecue sauce on the jackfruit mixed with the scent of Brady's fresh baked cinnamon gooey-goodness made my mouth water.

Brady scratched at a nick in the red table top with his thumbnail. "I rarely do." He looked up at me. "Mind Sunny, that is."

"You were telling me what you like?"

He leaned forward. His voice lowered. "Was I? I think Sunny covered the highlights."

"Mr. Corman, are you flirting with me?"

"Maybe."

"So, you are attracted to me," I accused a little too loudly.

Brady leaned sideways. He stared at Jo Jo, who was in the middle of taking an order. When Jo Jo didn't look back, Brady shrugged. "I have two eyes. Both work. Of course, I find you attractive."

"Do tell."

"Another time, perhaps. I have to get to a job out in Stony Park Villa."

"What kind of job?"

"I have to finish a screened-in porch I just built. All that's left is the screen and some trim." He slid out of the booth and stood up. He placed a five-dollar bill on the table near his unfinished cinnamon roll.

"Is it a rush job?" Or was he rushing to get away from me?

Brady slipped his wallet back into his jeans. "The customer is...difficult." Evelyn Meyers blew into Sunny's like a bitter wind. "Speak of the devil," Brady muttered.

"I'd probably strangle that woman if I had to work for her," I said.

"The thought's crossed my mind once or ten times."

Another woman with curly brown hair came in right behind the witch. I recognized her as one of the Hamlet cast. Right now, she looked like she was about to cry. "Ms. Meyers, please," she said. "Give me one more week."

"I'm trying to order coffeecake, Sabrina."

"I have a son," the woman pleaded.

21

"If I make an exception for you, I'd have to make an exception for all my renters." Evelyn turned back to Sunny who watched them both from behind the counter. "You got that cake ready yet?"

Sunny handed Evelyn a box with a twine bow on top. "Here you go, Ms. Meyers. That'll be twelve dollars and fifty cents."

Evelyn scoffed as she slid a twenty across to Sunny. "I can get the same cake from Walmart for under five dollars."

Sunny gave her a tight smile and handed Evelyn back her change. "That's great news. I hope you have a nice trip to Lake Ozarks."

The crotchety raccoon shifter grabbed her change and the boxed cake with a loud harrumph before leaving. The air in the cafe was immediately lighter. I got the impression Evelyn spent her waking hours darkening the lives of other people.

"Can I do something for you, Sabrina?" Sunny asked.

The young woman's voice was filled with defeat. "Can you figure out a way for me to come up with a thousand dollars in the next ten minutes?"

Sunny placed her hand over Sabrina's. She closed her eyes for a second and said, "You should ask for help."

"I wouldn't even know where to begin," Sabrina said. "But thank you for caring."

I looked at Brady. "Sunny sure has a way with people."

"Yes, she does." Brady nodded his head to me. "It's nice to see you again, Willy."

"Yeah?" I stood up, the top of my head barely at his

22

chin. I tilted my head back, enjoying the feel of his body heat so close to me.

He inhaled, his eyes half-closed. "Yes."

"You heading out, Dad?" Jo Jo asked, breaking the building tension between Brady and me.

"Yep." Brady took a step around me. "You'll be home for supper tonight?"

"Can't," Jo Jo said. "Rehearsal tonight."

"All right." Brady smiled at his son. "You tell Michele I said hello."

Jo Jo's face pinched. "We're not seeing each other anymore."

"Uh huh."

Sunny came back to the booth. "Hey, girl. I am getting slammed. How about we have dinner at the Blonde Bear after my play rehearsal tonight?"

"Sure. It's a date."

Brady left as I made plans with Sunny. It seemed I was destined to watch that man leave.

"Don't worry, Willy. Things have a way of working themselves out." Sunny squeezed my shoulder. "I better get back to work."

Since I'd lost all of my lunch companions, I finished my burger and headed out. I loved walking around Peculiar. The sounds of town folk chatting and the occasional roar of a dual exhaust pickup truck were the only real noises at combat with birds singing, chirping crickets, and all the other pleasant noises associated with rural living.

A few blocks past the courthouse, I found myself standing outside the police station. I didn't like being in

Peculiar on official Tri-State Council business and not notifying the sheriff or the mayor but considering Sunny was married to one and friends with the other, it was counterproductive to let them know I'd been sent to investigate her. Down the street, I watched Evelyn Meyers leave Dolly's Beauty Shop. Her hair didn't look much different, so she probably had some other beautification done.

A black muscle car with tinted windows roared past Evelyn, swerving left, its wheels clipping the curb next to the woman. She shrieked and stumbled back, falling to her rear end, but managing to save her newly purchased coffeecake, as the car righted itself and sped off.

I ran across the street. "Are you all right?" I held my hand out, and Evelyn took it. I pulled her to her feet.

She shook with adrenaline and fear. "Did you see that?"

"Do you know who it was? Did you see the driver?"

"No." She breathed noisily as her adrenaline waned.

"I caught part of the license plate. We should go file a police report."

Evelyn yanked her hand away from me. "No. I don't want to do that. I'm fine. I'm probably just overreacting."

"That car jumped the curb at you."

"It was probably some teenager on their cell phone."

"Still..."

"Drop it, Ms. Boden." Evelyn dusted her buttocks. "It's over now."

"I'd feel better filing a report."

She snarled, "Have a nice day." Leave it to Evelyn to make "Have a nice day," sound like, "Go to hell."

"Yeah, you too."

CHAPTER THREE

*B*efore dinner, Ruth had to deal with a crisis of teenage proportions. Michele had left her phone at the community center, and she couldn't possibly babysit Linus without it. What if she missed an important call? Blah, blah, drama, drama.

"Where did you leave your phone?" Ruth asked Michele.

"Backstage in the dressing area at the community center."

"Michele Margaret Thompson!"

"I didn't mean to leave it," the girl said defensively. "I went back just a few minutes after everyone left and the building was locked."

"You can live without your phone for one night, can't you?" Ruth asked. "It's not like we don't have a house phone."

Michele, who had the same Tinkerbell-like features

that marked her mother's beauty, balled her fists and shook them in the air. "It's not the same, Mom."

"Use the computer if you want to check your social media. The phone can wait."

"Roger's supposed to call me!" Michele slapped her hands over her mouth.

"Roger Parks?" Ruth's brown eyes narrowed on her daughter. "That boy is a thug."

"He's not, Mom," Michele protested. "He's really nice. At least, he's nice to me. I told him he could call me tonight. Please."

I didn't know Roger Parks from Adam, but I'm sure I'd get an earful later.

"And what do you want me to do?"

"Maybe you can ask Sunny to let you in tonight, and you can drop it off before you head to dinner?"

"You're almost twenty-years-old, Michele Margaret. Your phone is your responsibility."

"I know." She rolled her eyes. "When you were my age you were married, working full time, and taking care of three kids."

Ruth sighed again. "Fine. I'll ask Sunny."

Michele squealed and kissed Ruth on the cheek. "Thanks, Mom. You're the best."

"Yay, for super mom," I said when Michele jogged up the stairs to her room.

Ruth plopped her chin into her palm, her elbow resting on the table. "I guess I better call Sunny. Maybe she can meet us at the center before dinner."

"You are a saint, Ruth. Saint Ruth. I don't know how

you manage running your own business and taking care of nine kids."

"Taylor and Tyler both take care of themselves now," she disagreed. "Dakota's pretty self-sufficient as well."

"It's still a lot."

Ruth smiled, her eyes growing wistful. "I love being a wife and mom, Willy. I wouldn't change a single solitary thing about my life. Or my kids."

"Fair enough." I rarely felt jealousy when it came to other women, but in Ruth's case, my chest twinged with envy. "You're a lucky woman."

"I am." She stood up. "Guess I better let Ed know I'm leaving early."

SUNNY MET us outside the community center. "Is this what I have to look forward to with Jude and Dawn?"

"Yes." Ruth laughed. "The job doesn't end when they hit eighteen."

"It did for my father," I said. Soon as I graduated, he gave me a thousand dollars and wished me a happy life. My father was a stern man, but he'd never been unfair. I'd appreciated the money and used it to put the first and last month's rent on an apartment. I'd been working as a store clerk since I'd turned sixteen, so it wasn't a hard transition to a forty-hour week job. He did the same with Hans. He believed in the sink or swim method to adulthood, and Hans and I learned to swim quickly.

Sunny put the key in and jiggled the door handle. "It's

not locked. Dang it, I know I locked the door after rehearsal. Bob Winston is going to kill me if someone breaks in on my watch."

"Bob is the president of the community center," Ruth explained.

Sunny opened the door. "Let's get the phone and get going. I don't like the feel of this place tonight."

We went inside. Shadows stretched out from the corners of the stage area giving the charming community center a seriously eerie feeling

Ruth looked at Sunny. "Are you getting a... feeling?"

Sunny shrugged and chewed her lower lip. "Nothing concrete."

"I have a feeling my stomach is going to eat itself if we don't get some dinner soon." I rubbed my arms. "Let's get Michele's phone and get the fuck out of here. Besides, this place is giving my goose bumps goose bumps."

Ruth giggled. "The phone is backstage. You all wait here, I'll be right back."

"This place is creepy at night," I said.

"No lie," Sunny agreed.

A rumpled red velvet curtain on the left side of the stage had a metal sword sticking out about three feet up. I recalled the part in Hamlet where the vengeful Danish prince pokes his sword through the closet curtain, thinking his stepfather is listening in on a conversation with his mother, but he accidentally kills Polonius, his friend Horatio's dad. It seemed a little weird that it was just staying up without any support unless somebody stuck it into a wall.

"What's that?" I pointed to the sword.

"It looks like Hamlet's foil. What's it doing sticking in the curtain?"

"Found it," Ruth shouted out.

"Awesome." I nibbled my fingernail. As a bobcat shifter, my nose wasn't nearly as honed as a wolf or a coyote. However, I was still a predator, and the closer I got to the curtain the more potent the scent of fresh blood. "Uhm, I think we might have a problem out here."

Ruth came springing out from the back. She held a purple sparkly smartphone in her hand. "The lengths we go through for our children," she said then looked at me. "What?"

Sunny put her hand out in front of me. "We should call the police."

"I investigate this kind of thing for a living," I told her. "Besides, we can't call the police until we know why we're calling."

Sunny and Ruth exchanged looks, but neither of them said more.

I carefully made my way to the weapon. It was actually poking out between the two curtains, not through. My impulse was to yank the blade from the wall, but after four years as an investigator slash security officer for the Tri-State Council, I knew better than to tamper with potential evidence. I eased back the curtain, the scent of a kill overwhelming my senses. Two sightless eyes stared at me, her mouth wide open, her swollen tongue protruding, her skin cherry red with anger. She looked completely surprised by her death—but honestly, who wouldn't be?

"Don't come closer," I told Ruth and Sunny. "Evelyn Meyers is back here, and she is one scary, dead bitch."

Ruth coughed. "Oh, mercy."

"Who would want her dead?" I asked.

Sunny frowned. "The line for who didn't want her dead would be shorter."

"Sunny!" Ruth said.

"Tell me it's not true. I tolerated the woman about as well as anyone, but she was not likable. At all. And the way she acted at rehearsal tonight, I swear she was on drugs? The good shit."

Ruth interrupted the conversation. "We should call the sheriff."

"Yes, of course. You give him a call. I'm going to look around a bit." I drew out my phone from my purse. I wanted to document the scene before the locals started stomping all over it. I could hear Ruth in the background as I made a quick video of the entire stage. Later, I could go over every inch of footage to see if I could find any clues to the killer. It's not that I thought Sheriff Taylor and his men weren't competent. I did. But Sid Taylor was the victim's brother-in-law, and in my experience, family muddied the water.

A couple minutes later, the screech of sirens broke the quiet. Ruth, who had been nervously fidgeting with her phone and checking it every two seconds, said unnecessarily, "They're here."

I put away my phone. I didn't want to chance they'd confiscate and erase my memory card. It's what I would have done if someone filmed my crime scene. Sunny raised her brow at me then shrugged. I was betting she wouldn't rat me out. With the way Evelyn had been positioned behind the curtain, pinned like a bug on a board, I couldn't get a better view. I assumed the weapon killed her, but I couldn't be sure without a closer look at her entire body.

"Where is she," Sheriff Taylor said when he came inside. Deputy Tyler Thompson, Ruth's other twin son, followed closely on his heels. The sheriff's grim face shook me. I remembered what it was like when I found out my ex had been a murder victim. I might have not loved him, but it was still hard to know someone close to me had died.

"She's behind the curtain." I held up my hand when he got close. "You might want to wait until the coroner gets here before you handle her. The way she's pinned up may not hold together if you start moving things around."

"Pinned up?"

I indicated the metal foil sticking out. "Like a bug." I instantly regretted letting my inner words make an outward appearance. "I'm sorry, Sid. I know she's your sister-in-law. Too many years investigating shit like this, I guess."

"I understand, Ms. Boden." The sheriff turned to his deputy. "We need to get lights set up in here. Call in Farraday to catalog the crime scene. I'll get Doc Smith down here."

"On it," Tyler said. He put his hands on Ruth's shoulders. "You okay, Mom?"

"I'm fine," she said. She briefly touched his cheek.

After going into detective mode, I hadn't given much thought to Ruth or Sunny. Ruth was pale and miserable,

Sunny's hands shook, and I was a total asshole. "I'm so sorry, you guys. Let's get you out of here." I gave Tyler a nod. "We'll be outside when you're ready to question us. Some air will do all of us some good."

Outside, Sunny slumped against the wall. "I guess we won't be getting dinner. Damn it. This was mommy's night out."

"I don't think Evelyn got killed just to ruin your night," Ruth said.

Sunny scoffed. "I wouldn't put it past her."

Ruth squeezed Sunny's forearm. "After all this is over, we can still catch dinner."

"I just want to go home and cuddle my husband and babies." She sighed. "I guess I'll have to cancel rehearsal this week. I'd hate for everyone to show up at a crime scene." She looked at me. "You should stop by the house tomorrow. You can see the kids, and we can catch up. You know, one on one." The way she said it made me suspect Sunny knew more about why I was here than she should.

"One o'clock?"

"Sure," Sunny said. "Sounds like a plan."

Tyler Thompson came out the door. "I'll get your statements then you'll be free to go."

CHAPTER FOUR

*A*bout ten o'clock, I'd told Ruth I was going for a drive to clear my head, and maybe, that had been the original plan. But parked down at the end of Brady Corman's driveway for two hours, headphones blasting soul-tugging music, I was certain a clutter-free head wasn't happening anytime soon. Why couldn't I get this stupid coyote out of my head? He had more baggage than an airport on Christmas Eve. My brain told me to run, get as far away from Brady as inhumanly possible, but my heart, my gut, and all my lady parts wanted to launch myself on top of him, and seduce him into submission.

I'd never been in his home, but the night of the Halloween party, I'd given him a ride home. We'd both run headfirst into a burning barn. Brady, because his son Jo Jo was trapped inside, and me because I had the opposite reaction to danger than I should. My father used to say I had "no self-preservation instinct." I like to think of myself as more thrill seeker than suicidal. Anyhow, the rescue had

33

got my adrenaline pumping, so when Jo Jo asked for his dad's car to take his date home, I'd offered Brady a ride.

Our conversation on the way had been energized, the way conversations can get when two people escape death together. When I'd pulled into his driveway, Brady thanked me, and I'd felt the, "I'm gonna kiss you," vibe from him. So, I just jumped right in there and laid one on him.

Gah! Talk about sizzle, that heat of the man's lips lit my loins like a match to gasoline.

Then, just as abruptly as I'd kissed him, he disengaged, opened the truck door saying, "I can't do this," and then closed the door behind him with a hard slam, and rushed into his house.

I'd never been so confused, hurt, turned on, and dejected all at the same time. Which is why I sat at the end of his driveway now, because our lunch earlier hadn't made me any less confused, hurt, turned on, and dejected. I wanted Brady the way I wanted air and food and water. In other words, I felt like I couldn't live without him. Was that strange? I thought so. I'd had a lot of lovers over the years, but not a one of them moved me like this cranky single dad. At least, I was pretty sure he was single, considering the way Ruth and Sunny pushed me at him.

The first time I saw Brady, last June when Jo Jo had been kidnapped with Ruth's daughter Michele, he'd gone to the police station to report his son missing. Luckily, we'd found Jo Jo and Michele later that night tied up in the woods no worse for wear. Brady's vulnerability, the way he worried for his child, had tugged on every girly string inside me. It hadn't hurt that he was incredibly hot in a young Jeffrey Dean Morgan way. (Yes, I'd gone through a Supernatural phase. No, I still wasn't over it.) He'd worn a wedding band at the police station, but at Halloween and today, he'd been without it. Why would any woman in her right mind leave a man like him?

I cranked up the volume on my mp3 player and launched into the chorus of "Love Hurts" by Nazareth, a favorite of my father's. When the driver side door of my truck opened, I tore out the earplugs and jump hard enough to hit my head on the cab roof. Considering how short I am, the maneuver was a feat. "Jeezus. H. Christ. You scared the ever-loving shit out of me!"

Brady appeared befuddled for a moment, but he managed a glower when he said, "You're the one scaring, well, everything out here. I thought someone was dying."

I blushed. "I have a fine singing voice."

"More like a cat yowling."

"You're being a jerk."

"You're parked on my road in the middle of the night."

"I'm parked off your road in the middle of the night."

"Fine." He shook his head. "What are you doing here, Willy?"

"I'm thinking."

"And you couldn't do that back in town?"

"I found a body tonight. You could be a little kinder to me." Besides, earlier he'd said it was nice to see me. Had something changed between then and now?

"What?" He dipped his head. "You found a body? Like an actual person?"

"No, like a fake person."

"Willy..."

"Yes, fine. An actual person."

"Who? Where?"

"Now all we need is the what and why, and the crime will have solved itself."

"So, it was a crime?" Alarm rose in his voice. "Someone was murdered?" He reached in and grabbed my arms. "Who?"

Damn it. I really was an asshole. Brady had lived in Peculiar his entire life. Of course, he'd be freaked out. It didn't help that he knew the victim. After all, he was building a screen porch for her. I hoped she'd paid him up front.

"It's Evelyn Meyers. Sunny, Ruth, and I found her dead at the community center tonight. I'm so sorry, Brady."

He ran his fingers through his thick, dark brown hair. His amber eyes glowing with his animal just below the surface. The hairs on the back of my neck stood up.

"Are you sure she was murdered?"

"She had a sword through the chest. I'm pretty sure she didn't do that to herself."

"How long ago?"

"I'm not sure. We were there at eight-thirty p.m., rehearsal was over by six, so it had to be sometime in that two and a half hour window. I'm sure Doc Smith will have more information after his autopsy."

"Billy Bob isn't going to share jack shit with me."

"He might with me. Why do you want to know when Evelyn died?"

"No reason."

"That's a load of crap, Brady. I know fishing when I hear it. Do you have any idea who wanted to kill her? I mean, other than half the town."

"No, not really."

I remembered Jo Jo's outburst at the center. "Is this about your son? Do you think he might have been angry enough to--"

"That's ridiculous." His brow furrowed, worry apparent.

I got out of the truck and put my hand on his forearm. Electric sparks shot up my fingertips and through my body. God, I hated and loved the way he made me feel. I removed my hand. "I'll keep close tabs on the investigation." Which I'd already planned to do, but I felt the need to reassure him.

Brady nodded. "Thanks." He ran his hand through his hair again. Oh, how I envied those fingers. He gave me that same, "I so wanna kiss you," look, but I didn't jump into his arms this time. Burn me twice, shame on me.

"I better get back before Ruth sends out the troops."

He raised a brow. "Ruth can be a real drill sergeant."

I recognized sarcasm when I heard it. "Well, really, I'm just trying hard not to scare you off again. Figured, I'd be the one to take off first this time."

Brady's eyes widened before a sly smile spread across his lips. "Yeah, sorry about that."

"Sorry for kissing me like you meant it, or sorry for running off?"

His Adam's apple bobbed once. Hot damn, I wanted to lick the nervous sweat off his neck. "Both."

"Explain."

He reached out and tucked a long curl of mine behind my ear. "You're nothing like her, you know."

"Who?"

"My wife."

Fuuuck! Was he still married? "I'm a goddamn home-wrecker. Jeezus, Brady. Why did you flirt with me? You don't even wear a freaking ring."

"I only stopped wearing the band last year." He fidgeted with his left ring finger. "Rose Ann died."

"Shit. I'm sorry, Brady. I didn't know." The way Sunny, Chavvah, and Ruth liked to gossip, I can't believe not one of them clued me into this tidbit of information. Although, I guess I could have asked. I think a part of me had been afraid to know the truth. "Was it recent?"

He shook his head. "Twelve years now, but until about two years ago, I didn't know how or why." He shook his head again. "It's a long story. One I'm not ready to talk about."

"Okay."

"I'd really like to kiss you again."

"But?" I waited for the other shoe to drop.

"I haven't been with anyone but my wife."

"Ever?" I hoped we weren't trading histories, because I lost my virginity at seventeen, and I'd never lived like a nun.

"Ever." He touched his ring finger again. "It feels a little like betrayal."

"Do you think Rose Ann would feel that way?"

He chuckled. "No. She was the kindest, most gentle person I'd ever met."

"So, my complete opposite."

Brady snorted. "Well, her other half was a mountain lion."

I smiled. "Aww, you like the kitties," I teased. "Sorry. I should probably keep the flirting to a minimum."

He dipped his head and inhaled my hair. "You smell like fresh cut grass on a sunny day."

"I hope you like fresh cut grass," I said. I tilted my head sideways, giving him access if he wanted to take advantage of my neck real estate.

When his lips grazed my skin, my whole body tensed at the jolt of pleasure. "Damn, woman, you're so beautiful." His fingertips stroked down my bare arms. He kissed my neck again. "I haven't wanted anyone, not like this, in a very long time."

I pressed my palms into his broad chest and sagged against him. "I want you, too, Brady."

The porch light came on. "Dad? You out there?"

Brady practically threw himself away from me. "I'm here. Be right in." He looked at me, his face stark as if he'd just seen a ghost. "I'm sorry, Willy. I...can we talk tomorrow?"

"Uh, sure. I'll try and find out more about Evelyn. And don't worry. Jo Jo's a good kid. I'm sure he didn't have anything to do with, you know." Cripes. Investigation 101. You didn't rule out suspects based on emotions. Just because I wanted Jo Jo to be innocent for Brady's sake didn't mean the kid wasn't guilty.

"I appreciate that." His lips tugged up at the corners in a sweet, simple smile. "I really do want to continue tonight's conversation at a later time."

Rawr. I flashed him a grin. "It's a date, hot stuff."

He laughed. My pulse raced. I waited for him to walk up the drive, appreciating the view, before I got in my truck and left. My neck still sizzled where Brady had trailed kisses. I wasn't used to slow-playing a man, and Brady was more damaged than the average guy, but I had a feeling he would be worth every agonizing moment I had to wait for him to be ready.

CHAPTER FIVE

*M*orning came early at the Thompson home. I heard the sounds of showers running, toilets flushing, girl's talking, boys walking, and the scent of bacon, pancakes, and fried eggs miraculously made its way to the second floor. I'd told Ruth I got up at seven o'clock, and on the hour, I heard one of the younger boys knock on my door and loudly proclaim, "Bathroom's free!"

I rolled up into a sitting position and swung my feet over the side of the bed. The freshly washed sheets had smelled like lavender, and I'd slept more soundly than I thought possible after the way the night had ended. I dressed, peed, washed my face, brushed my teeth, finger combed my messy curls and headed down to the kitchen where I prayed a strong black cup of coffee waited for me. Mornings were the only time I indulged.

"Morning," I said as Ruth greeted me with a smile and a

mug. Yay! Coffee. I took a sip. Mmm mmm. "Breakfast smells great."

Ed was sitting at the table reading a newspaper. God, I loved small town living. So much simpler than city life where every bit of news came through the internet. He had the classic deer shifter features, thin face, high cheeks, and wide large brown eyes. His sandy blond hair was short and combed neatly. He wore a blue t-shirt and jeans with grease stains, and steel tipped work boots. I noticed Ruth was wearing similar attire.

"Gotta go into the shop with Ed today. I have to rebuild a carburetor on an F150. It was an unexpected order, and Ed has to go into Lake Ozarks for a couple of cases of 10W40."

I gave her a bland look.

"Motor oil for performance cars. We could order it in, but after shipping costs, it's cheaper for the customer and us to drive the thirty miles to pick it up."

"Ah," I said. "That's fine. I wanted to go talk to the sheriff this morning anyhow, and I have that lunch date with Sunny this afternoon. I can keep myself busy."

A small boy with the same color hair as his father streaked naked through the kitchen. He squealed with joy as he ran around the table back to the living room and up the stairs.

"Linus!" Ruth hollered. "Get your clothes on, boy. You come back down here naked and I'm feeding your share of bacon and pancakes to Leroy and Emma Ray."

"Noooooo!" I heard him cry out.

To me, she said, "I'm so sorry, Willy. He's a free spirit."

I laughed and waved away her apology. "I barely saw a thing." Besides, it wasn't like therianthropes were known for their modesty. We had to undress to shift, and when we shifted back, we were still naked. The fact that Ruth thought anything of Linus being naked surprised me. It was an almost human reaction. "Breakfast smells awesome." Louder, I said, "If we're giving away bacon and pancakes, I want in on that."

Linus ran into the kitchen wearing red shorts and a purple tank top. "I'm dressed," he announced. "No giving away my food."

Ruth ruffled his hair. "Go get your brother and sisters. Tell them to move their feet or lose their meat."

Linus giggled, and it was such a pleasant sound. "Yes, ma'am."

"You've got good kids, Ruth."

Ed, who hadn't uttered a word since I'd come down, put his paper down, and smiled. "The best," he agreed. "But with a mom like Ruth, how could they be anything less."

He grabbed his wife by the hand and pulled her down on his lap. They kissed, sweet and soft. Again, the familiar twinge of envy pinched my chest. "You all should come with a cavity warning," I teased, but it was nice to see that sparks could still fly after twenty-three years of marriage.

After breakfast, I walked to the police station. It was a warm summer morning, and like most cats, I loved the feel of the sun on my skin.

"Willy," Deputy Connelly said. "What are you doing in Peculiar? Council business?"

"No," I replied a little too quickly. "I'm here for a visit. Unfortunately, I found Evelyn Meyers last night with Ruth Thompson and Sunny Trimmel."

"Bad business, that. The woman could be a terror, but I never actually thought someone would bump her off."

"That's why I stopped by. A car tried to run her down yesterday afternoon. It went up on the sidewalk and took a swipe at her. I didn't think of it until late last night."

Deputy Connelly's expression turned serious. "Let's go have a seat." I followed him to his desk. It was as skeleton crew today, which didn't surprise me, considering Sheriff Taylor probably had most his deputies on duty last night with the crime scene. Still, I saw Sid in his office and gave him a nod when the deputy and I passed by.

Connelly woke his computer up. "Hold on. It'll take me a second to pull up a witness statement."

"Take your time." I looked around the room. There were five desks with desktop computers, a bookshelf with procedural manuals, and a copy machine. There were three labeled doors, one was the File Room, another Evidence Lock Up, and the final door was the Armory.

"Here it is," Connelly said.

"Where's the interrogation room?"

"What?"

"The place you take suspects to interrogate them."

Connelly laughed. "We rarely have serious enough crimes to have to interrogate anyone. However, when we do, we have a small room down the hall off the break room."

"Cool."

"Now, where did you see this car when it swerved to hit Ms. Meyers?"

"Out in front of Dolly's Beauty Shop."

"When was this?"

"Around one-forty-five. I'd finished eating at Sunny's Outlook around one-thirty and walked down this way. I was standing outside your building as a matter of fact when I saw it go down."

"Did you recognize the driver?"

"Unfortunately, the windows were heavily tinted. I couldn't make out the driver."

"What kind of vehicle?"

"It was a black two-door muscle car. One of those boxy numbers. I got a partial license plate number when it passed me, but after it swerved up on the curb, I stopped looking at the car and started running toward Evelyn who'd fallen on the sidewalk."

"What did you get from the plates?"

"The first three letters were ERG. Missouri plate." I shook my head. "I wonder if Evelyn's death might have been prevented if she'd just reported the incident."

"Why didn't she?"

"I don't know. I offered to come into the station with her to give a witness statement, but she insisted that it had just been a reckless accident." I met Connelly's gaze. "I saw the car. It purposefully turned toward Evelyn."

"Would you recognize the car if you saw it again?"

"I would."

"Is there anything else you can remember about the incident."

"No," I said. I took one of Connelly's cards off his desk. "If I remember something else, I'll give you a call." I noticed a picture of him in a tuxedo next to a white-gowned buxom woman with golden-brown hair. "Congratulations."

"Thanks." He held up his left hand to show me his wedding band. He beamed with enormous pride. "Four months now."

"You make a cute couple," I told him. I thought about Brady and his lack of a ring. "What do you know about the death of Rose Ann Corman?"

Connelly shook his head. "Too much." He rubbed his face. "She was the first victim of that hunter group. She'd worked for Neville Lutjen as his assistant. Brady was the mayor then."

"Brady Corman?"

"Yes." The deputy laughed at me. "Your face is priceless. Yes, Brady Corman was our mayor for almost a decade before Lutjen. His wife's disappearance drove him down a dark path. He lost almost everything. He's lucky he didn't lose Jo Jo."

"Deputy Connelly," Sheriff Taylor said. "I don't pay you for idle gossip."

"It's my fault," I said.

Connelly changed the conversation. "Willy saw a car try to hit Evelyn Meyers yesterday afternoon in front of Dolly's." The weresquirrel might look slow, but he knew how to recover from a bad situation.

The sheriff's lips thinned in a grimace. "Do we know who was driving?"

The deputy shook his head. "Not yet, but there can't be that many black muscle cars in town."

"If you need an extra set of eyes or ears, Sheriff Taylor, I'm happy to help out."

"I'll let you know," he said. "I'm still waiting on Doc Smith to get back to me with an autopsy report." The skin around Sheriff Taylor's eyes always looked a little dark. It was a common phenomenon in raccoon shifters, but today his circles had circles.

"How's Jean holding up?" It had to be hard losing a sister, even one as repugnant as Evelyn.

"My daughter is home with her."

It wasn't really an answer. "I didn't know you had a daughter."

"Nicole," he said. His eyes brightened. "She's home for the summer. She just finished her Ph.D. at Stanford."

Not even murder could put a damper on his fatherly pride. "Impressive."

"She's gifted. Always has been." He leaned against a support beam next to Connelly's desk. "It's going to be hard on Jean when she leaves again."

"She might stick around more now that school's out," the deputy said. His words lacked conviction. "You never know."

"She'll be busier than ever," Sheriff Taylor said. "And that's okay. Anyways, I thank you for coming in this morning, Willy, but we got it from here. You go enjoy your vacation." He emphasized "vacation" as if putting finger quotes around the word. "We've got more than enough people working on this investigation."

"Thanks. I'll do that."

As I was leaving, I remembered the encounter between Evelyn and Sabrina at Sunny's Outlook. I almost turned around. Almost. It was a public confrontation, and since Sid had "more than enough people" working the investigation, I was certain it wouldn't take them long to track down suspects.

I still had a few hours before I had to meet with Sunny. I went back to Ruth's and got my car. Brady had said he'd been building a screen porch for the victim at Stony Park Villa. It probably wouldn't come to anything, but it might be worth a look to see where Evelyn Meyers lived. My going to her house had absolutely nothing to do with the fact that Brady might be there gathering any leftover equipment.

CHAPTER SIX

$\mathcal{I}$ used the GPS on my phone to find Stony Park Villa. It was a small cul-de-sac subdivision with six homes in a large circle. Each large split-level house sat on two to three acres of land, and each one had a three-car garage. There were minor differences in architecture, and no two homes were the same color. Three of the yards had been recently seeded with new grass. One still had freshly dozed dirt everywhere and a "For Sale" sign. The last two had manicured lawns that had seen at least one summer.

Now, if I were Evelyn Meyer's house, which house would I be?

The easiest solution was to look in the backyards and find the screened-in porch. I pulled in front of the house surrounded by dirt. It didn't look occupied, so I hoped the neighbors would assume I was a potential buyer and not call the cops on me for snooping.

I got out of the truck, disappointed when I didn't see

any sign of Brady. I pulled the back of the seat forward and grabbed my work backpack. I checked inside. Pocket flashlight, baggie with nitrile gloves, lock pick set, scissors, Swiss Army knife, pens, notepad, sanitizer wipes, doggie treats (you never knew when bribing a dog might come in handy), granola bars, beef jerky, and trail mix (you never knew when a snack attack would happen on a stakeout), shoe booties, and a hair net. I grabbed my phone from my purse and dropped it into the front pocket of the bag. The advent of smartphones had made recording devices and cameras for documenting an investigation unnecessary.

It was close to ten a.m., and the street was quiet. School was out for summer, but there were no children running around. I walked behind the empty house. There was an open deck. Pretty basic. And no construction.

I moved toward the fence line and walked counterclockwise. One of the established yards, the blue house with brown trim, had a double deck and a gazebo. Nice, but not the place I was looking for. It took a couple of minutes to get to the next yard. A tan house, white trim, in a recently seeded yard. There were still some sporadic spots of loose straw on bare patches. Low and behold, there was a screened-in porch. Finished even, which meant Brady had most likely finished the work yesterday afternoon and cleaned up before leaving. Too bad Evelyn would never get a chance to enjoy the new digs.

The porch itself wasn't locked up. Good for me. The neighbors wouldn't be able to see me break and enter through the back door. Jeezus, why was I doing this? Besides my natural curiosity, I wanted to give Brady reassurance that his son wasn't a killer. Was I being presumptuous? Hell yes.

Two large ceiling fans with wicker blades circulated air over a wicker loveseat, two chairs, a lounger, and a table with four chairs. A few ants crawled on the table. A fine layer of dust covered the entire glass top except for two rings the size of silver dollars, and the word "Bitch" spelled out in capital letters. Someone made a house call.

Crap. Brady built this porch. Was he the dust writer? I'd met Evelyn, and if she hadn't been killed the night before I might have been tempted to write the word in her dust but I didn't want to believe it of Brady. It seemed out of character for the man, but truthfully, what did I know about him other than he made my hormones dance a jig whenever he was near? That wasn't enough to say he was of good moral fiber. Let's face it, my taste in men had always been suspect. I'd picked some real losers over the years.

I checked the back door. It was a standard keyed-door lever. Not one of the most secure locks on the planet.

I put on my hair net to harness my curls. Wouldn't do to have red strands of hair all over the place when Sheriff Taylor and his deputies got around to processing Evelyn's house. Next, I pulled on a pair of nitrile gloves, slipped the shoe covers on my tennis shoes, and grabbed my lock pick set from my backpack.

Hmm. People in the city wouldn't leave their homes unsecured, but I grew up in a rural area and knew small-town folks rarely locked their doors. However, there were tool marks on the key entry. Someone had come before me. I tested the handle, and it turned. Bingo. I put away my pick set and went inside.

The back door led directly into Evelyn's modern kitchen. The counters were black marble, and the appliances were stainless steel. She had a center island with a sink, two rinsed tea cups and some forks sitting inside, and a grill. Over the top was an exhaust fan that traveled up to the vaulted ceiling. Copper bottom pots hung from a stainless steel lighted pot rack, but weirdly, I couldn't smell a hint of food. She didn't have any of the telltale signs of a cook, even though her kitchen would make a professional chef salivate.

I opened the refrigerator and saw a couple blocks of cheese, an open bottle of wine, a Sunny's Outlook box, some deli ham, and a jar of mayo. I opened the Sunny's Outlook box. It was the coffee cake Evelyn had picked up yesterday afternoon. Two pieces were missing, which meant Evelyn had come home long enough before rehearsals to eat two pieces of cake or she shared them with someone. Either way, Evelyn came home before rehearsals.

A sudden pang twisted my gut. Had she shared the cake with Brady? Oh, crap. Would Sheriff Taylor see Brady as a suspect? I couldn't see a motive, but he clearly had access to the woman. I knew he hadn't done it, though. He'd been genuinely surprised when I'd told him about Evelyn's death, but he'd also been worried Jo Jo might be involved. If my hormones hadn't fogged my brain, I would've asked. The next time I saw Brady, I'd have to ask.

My phone rang, and I nearly jumped up on the center

island. I fished it from my backpack. Sunny's name flashed on the screen. I composed myself and answered on the third ring. "Hey, girl," I said. "We're still on this afternoon. Right?"

"Of course," Sunny said. "I'm looking forward to it, which is why I called. You have about ten minutes to get out of Evelyn Meyer's home before the sheriff gets there. Oh, and FYI, the drawer in her office desk has a false bottom. See you at one!" She hung up.

I stood there for about two seconds with my mouth agape. I ran to the living room and peeked out the curtains. How could Sunny possibly know I was at Evelyn's house or that the sheriff was going to be here? I supposed someone could have told her about the sheriff coming to check out the victim's house. After all, her husband was the town's mayor, but no one knew I was here. No one.

I really liked Sunny, and I hated that I'd been directed to spy on her, but she was kind of scaring me. Okay, if I believed her, then I had about five minutes to give the house a once over and get the heck out. It wouldn't be great if Sid Taylor recognized my truck leaving the cul-de-sac, but it would be even worse if he caught me rummaging through a dead woman's house.

The living room, much like the kitchen was über modern. For a woman who ran an antique store, there was a distinct lack of antiques in her home. I don't know why I had expected Evelyn's style to be more traditional country or lady of the manor. But everything about her home felt cold and impersonal, much like the woman herself. On the wall in her hallway was a framed picture of a much younger

Evelyn with Jean, and two people who I assumed were their parents. They all smiled, but not a one of them seemed happy. The house was two stories, which meant I wouldn't be able to go through the whole thing in the allotted time, but according to Sunny, there was one place I definitely had to check, so I just started opening and closing doors until I found the important room. The office had a desk with a computer, an old fashioned ten-key, bank books, and a landline handset phone with answering machine. The only item not business related was a bird figurine with a vivid green and blue body, and a peach face. It reminded me of a parrot, but the beak was too small. Since it was a figurine, there was no telling how large the bird was in real life or even if it had been modeled after a real bird.

The answering machine surprised me. Hardly anyone had them anymore. There was one message. I pushed the button. Jean Taylor's voice came on. "Evie, you can't keep ignoring me. I know you've been in touch with Nicole. Give me a call so we can talk about it."

And that was it. Frankly, Jean didn't even sound angry. So much for the proverbial answering machine lead. I opened the top middle drawer. It had the usual organized sections of staples, thumbtacks, paper clips, sticky notes, scissors, and such. I pulled the drawer out far enough to lift the organizer. It came right up.

"Hm," I grunted. In the false bottom, there was a brown leather-bound accounts ledger. There were transactions with dates of deposits, payouts, withdrawals, and so on that all seemed to go to fruit. Mango, Plum, Blueberries, Peaches, and more. The Big Grape seemed to get the most attention, but nothing to identify where the money came from or who it was going out to, I took pictures with my phone one page after another. The balance at the bottom of the last page stuck out to me immediately. *$985,450* was scribbled in the total column.

Christ, did Evelyn have almost a million dollars in the bank? How did a small town antique store owner have that kind of money? Did she make really wise investments into fruit? I looked at my phone again. Crappola. I needed to go. I put the ledger back, because it might be evidence, and the last thing I wanted to do was impede Sid's investigation. After, I closed all the doors I'd opened and made sure I hadn't moved anything or left any trace of myself behind then skedaddled out the door.

I ducked down a little in my seat when I passed the sheriff's SUV on the way out of Stony Park Villa. *Shii-it*. I'd got out barely in the nick of time. I pulled out my phone and dialed Sunny.

"Hey, Willy," she said brightly. "What's up?"

"You mind if I come early? I think we need to talk sooner rather than later."

"I already have soup on the stove and some sourdough bread in the oven. I hope you're hungry."

I blanched. "Actually, I'm famished."

CHAPTER SEVEN

*S*unny and Babe's cabin was a small two-bedroom place out in the country. The yard was a little overgrown. Wildflowers popped up all over the setting, lending splotches of color to the place. It was messy and beautiful all at the same time. Sunny's SUV was parked in the gravel drive. She sat out on the porch swing and waved as I pulled in and parked behind her vehicle.

Her son Jude ran around with his arms out making airplane noises, and Dawn, who wasn't a year old yet, sat content in Sunny's lap. "Come on over and have a seat," she said, looking every bit a mom. "Dawn won't bite." She laughed and tickled her daughter's tummy. "Well, she might, but I'll protect you." The baby girl giggled.

Shifter children matured slower than human children, so Dawn, who was a little over six months old, looked like a three-month-old human.

I sat down next to Sunny. She stared at me expectantly, and I found that Dawn wasn't the only one squirming. I remembered that it had taken Jude four months for his first shift. It wasn't unheard of, but it was rare. Most therianthropes shifted on their first full moon, no matter their age. "Has she shifted, yet?"

"Yes." Sunny beamed with pride. "She was three weeks old on the first full moon. She went all furry and yipped like crazy. Coyote pups are adorable."

I gave her a quizzical look. Could she remember her full moon shifts? I'd never heard of that happening. On the full moon, our animal forms dominated our human forms. It was the only time when we operated on pure instinct. I could recall scents and emotions from my shifts during a moon cycle, but I'd never had any concrete memories.

Maybe she wasn't talking about Dawn's first shift. She could have seen the little girl shift anytime. It wasn't like we were confined to only shifting with the full moon, and the rest of the time, we could think and process like a human, even if our senses were more heightened.

"Sunny, how did you know I was at her house? What's going on that you're not telling me?"

Her bow lips tugged up into a smile. "Am I a suspect, Willy? Do you think I had something to do with Evelyn Meyer's death?"

"Of course not." I didn't suspect Sunny at all, but she knew stuff she shouldn't know. "You told that Sabrina chick to ask for help. Why?"

"We can all use a little help from time to time."

"Did you know Evelyn was going to die? Are you covering for someone?"

"No, I didn't know Evelyn was going to die. As to the second question, I have no idea who killed her."

"Then how?"

Dawn wiggled around and sprouted fur, a muzzle, and a tail. Sunny took off what was left of the baby's diaper and put the coyote pup down to join her brother. She turned her gaze on me. "That's the question, right? You're here to find out more about me?"

"Jeezus, Sunny, what are you some kind of mind reader?"

"Some kind," she said seriously.

"I...what? Are you saying you can read minds?"

She laughed. "Don't you worry, Wilhelmina Boden, your secrets are safe with me. I don't read minds. I mean, occasionally I'll get a phrase or a word here or there, but mostly, I just see things happen. It might be a past event, something in the present, or something that has yet to happen."

"Are you yanking my chain?"

Sunny leaned over and looked at my back. "Nope," she said. "Your chain remains unyanked."

"You're a seer then, is that what you're saying?"

"I am a psychic. Not a very good one. And let me tell you, when I was pregnant, my ability was non-existent, but since Dawn's birth, it's gotten pretty much back to normal."

"A psychic?" I scoffed. "I've never heard of a theri-anthrope psychic before. If a person like you existed in our world, believe me, I would have heard about it." I studied every species of therians and lycans in the United States after the Tri-State Council hired me.

"Well, that's the rub," Sunny said. "And it's the thing you're here for. I'm not a therianthrope."

"Lycanthrope?"

Sunny chuckled. "Billy Bob and Chavvah are the only two werewolves in town." Her eyes were almost sad when she looked at me. "I'm human, Willy."

"You can't be."

"But I am. I'm a human psychic living in a therian community. Is it against the Tri-State Council rules? Yes. So, I suppose what happens next is up to you. I've already discussed it with Babe, and we'll be okay whatever you decide." She took my hand and gave it a pat. "I like you, Willy. I'd like to be your friend, but you can't be friends with someone who you can't be honest with."

"Fuck my life," I said.

"It's a pretty good life." Sunny patted my leg and stood up. "Come on, Jude. Dawn. It's time for lunch." She looked down at me. "You coming in?"

"If you're psychic then you already know."

"I have four bowls set on the table."

I rolled my eyes. "I'm coming." This was a lot to process, but I could smell the black bean soup from out here, and I was hungry.

Sunny's kitchen was sage green. Above a copper back-splash, the words "Above all else. Love." had been stenciled on the wall. Dawn had changed back into human form. Sunny put another diaper on her and strapped her into a high chair. Jude, who was small, but mobile, sat in a chair with a booster seat. "Yummy," he squealed when Sunny put a bowl down in front of him that had been sitting on the counter when we got inside.

"I let his bowl cool down while we were outside." Dawn got a bowl of rice cereal and a sippy cup of watered-down juice. There were two pots on the stove. Sunny dished my bowl from one and hers from the other.

I raised a brow. "What's the difference?"

"Mine is vegetarian," she said. "Yours has cubed chicken breast. I can't eat meat."

"Can't or won't?"

"When I eat meat, I experience the last moments of the poor animal's life. Nothing kills the appetite like pain, gore, and death."

"That's part of your psychic thing." I spooned up a mouthful of soup. Spicy, earthy, with a hint of lime and cilantro. "Hot damn, this is delicious."

"I do own a restaurant."

"But I've never eaten any of your food with meat in it." I laughed and took another bite.

"My babies are carnivores, so I have to compromise at home."

"Well, it's good."

"Thanks."

"You knew Evelyn sent the Tri-State Council a note about you?"

Sunny shook her head and blew the steam off her spoon. "It doesn't surprise me that it was Evelyn, but no, I didn't know. I did have a vision of you sitting in an office with a short man with waxy blond hair and a porn-stache ordering you to Peculiar to investigate me."

I guffawed. "That would be Richard Stenson. He's the new president since Lowry stepped down. He's an opossum therianthrope, and he's been with the council for twelve years. A hard man, but fair. Still," I giggled, "he does have a porn-stache. I want to hand him a jar of shaving cream and razor every time I'm summoned to his office." I shook my head. "There's no way you could have known Stenson sent me. Usually, my orders come from lower on the power pole."

"I also saw you at Blonde Bear Cafe with Brady Corman. The chemistry between you was electric."

"Well, that definitely hasn't happened."

"Yet."

I dipped my sourdough bread into my soup and let it soak up the juices as I pondered Sunny's revelation. "I'm not sure things are going anywhere with Brady."

"Why?" She dipped her bread and took a bite.

"I think he might be hung up on a ghost."

"Rose Ann isn't a ghost. At least not anymore."

I choked on my bite of food. "I didn't mean literally. You see ghosts?"

"Only shifter ghosts, apparently." She shuddered and rubbed her arms. "Judah, Babe's brother, showed me what those hunters did to him and those other men." She took a deep breath. "And Rose Ann. I hate to even think about what would have happened to Chav if we hadn't found her. Well, I got kidnapped by the assholes, but that's beside the point. I am just glad I was able to help all those victims finally find peace."

I didn't know what to think about Sunny's proclamation of psychic abilities and seeing shifter ghosts, but I did have a question burning inside me. "What do you know about Rose Ann?"

"She was agreeable for a ghost. From what Jo Jo has told me, she was the glue in their family. When she disappeared, Brady thought she'd run off on him. It destroyed him. I think he still holds on to the shame of those years. Rose Ann was able to say goodbye to her family through me, but for Brady, that meant she also was able to see the mess he'd made of his life. The mess he'd made of being a father to their son." Sunny's eyes teared up. "All those wasted years of hate and bitterness. I'm afraid he's overcompensating these days. The problem is, Jo Jo doesn't need him the same way. I worry his guilt is going to keep him from having anything good in his life."

My heart ached for Brady, for Jo Jo, and even for Rose Ann, as Sunny talked about them. How could he ever be mine if he was still clinging to his dead wife? If she still held that kind of sway over him?

"I'd like to talk to Doc Smith today about Evelyn. I might be able to help with the case. Do you think he'd speak to me?"

Sunny nodded. "I'll call Chav. He'll talk to you if she asks him."

"I appreciate it." Brady might not be ready for a relationship, but it wasn't going to stop me from fulfilling my promise to him.

Sunny got up from her seat, walked over to me, and gave me a hug. "Thanks," she said.

"For what?"

"For keeping my secret."

"I haven't made up my mind what to do yet."

She grinned. "Yes, you have."

I shook my head. "Balls." She was right. I had.

"Balls!" Jude yelled. "Balls, balls, balls!"

I gave Sunny a guilty look. "At least I didn't say something worse."

My phone rang. Sunny said, "Tell Brady I said hello."

I looked at the screen. My stomach fluttered. "Hey," I said when I answered.

"Hey," Brady said back. "You want to have dinner with me tonight?"

"Uhm." I shook my head at Sunny. "Sure. Where and when?"

"Is the Blonde Bear Cafe okay? I can pick you up at Ruth's around six-thirty."

I widened my eyes at Sunny. She really was psychic. "Yeah, great. I'll be ready."

I stood up and looked at Sunny. "I guess I have a date tonight. Does it end well?"

"I'm not a fan of spoilers," Sunny said. She winked. "I'll call Chav now. You head on out to the clinic." She wiped Dawn's face. "I know two little coyotes who need baths and afternoon naps!"

"Before I go." I paused. I'd never believed in psychics, but for whatever reason, my instincts and my heart told me Sunny was the real deal. "Do you have any idea who killed Evelyn Meyers?"

She shook her head. "Sorry. I told you I was a bad psychic, right? I get the feeling though, that whoever stabbed her felt justified. I got the impression that the act of running a sword through Evelyn made the murderer sick to his or her stomach."

"You've been working closely with her for the past couple of weeks. Any suspects jump out at you?"

"I wish there were fewer suspects and more mourners. That woman wasn't liked. At all."

"She had a lot of money. I know she owned an antique store, but it couldn't possibly make the kind of money Evelyn had."

Sunny shrugged. "She owns a couple of duplexes. You might ask Milo Greene. He's the bank manager. I think they were neighbors, too."

Greene sounded like he could provide the right information, but I wasn't sure he'd talk to me.

"Just flash him your Tri-State Council badge. I think you'll find it holds some weight with the elders in the community."

I gave Sunny a curious look. "You're a good friend to have, Sunny Trimmel."

She grinned. "Yes. Yes, I am."

CHAPTER EIGHT

*D*octor Smith's clinic was just north of town past the bridge leading into Peculiar. As I drove down the gravel road, I passed a yurt-like structure on the left. The outside walls might have been made with tanned hides or canvas, I couldn't tell from the distance, and I was not an expert anyhow. At the top of a hill on the right, there was a sign that said, "Peculiar Medical Center Parking." Four vehicles were parked there, three trucks and a mid-size car. A covered porch spanned about thirty feet on the very long ranch-style building, and when I pulled in, I saw a door that said, "Clinic Entrance."

On the way, I'd called Richard Stenson and told him that I couldn't find anything strange with Sunny. I didn't like lying, but I would have liked exposing Sunny even less. I told him about Evelyn Meyers' murder, mostly to move the subject off my psychic friend. His voice was strained when he ordered me to find out more about her death. I agreed, of course, since I was already investigating. He wouldn't tell me why a small-town woman's death mattered to the Tri-State Council, and I was smart enough to let shit pass, especially when it served my own interest.

When I turned off the ignition to my truck, I felt rather pleased with myself. I was now on official Tri-State Council business. It gave me a card to play if anyone, like the sheriff, tried to block me from the investigation. Sunny had told me that the doctor's clinic was attached to his home, so I figured the security door on the right side had to be the personal entrance. It was only three-fifteen, which meant the clinic would still be open. I hated to bother Doc Smith during business hours, but I had to find out the official cause of Evelyn's death.

I walked in. On either side of a waiting area, two cushioned benches were affixed to the walls. A man with a wrapped hand sat in one corner. A teenager picked his nose and played on his phone. He sat next to Sabrina, the desperate young woman from Sunny's Outlook. She absently twirled one of her brown curls around her finger. Next to them was another woman with straight black hair, pale skin, and barely-blue pale eyes. She read a book on her tablet. At the front of the waiting area, next to another door, was a small counter in a window with a sign-in sheet. I wasn't there for an appointment, and since no one manned the counter, I wasn't sure how to go about getting the doc's attention.

"Is somebody working here?" I asked the raven-haired woman.

She blinked up at me. "Yeah, the doc."

"I mean like a secretary."

She smiled. "Doc Smith doesn't have a secretary. He'll be out in a bit. Just sign in."

"But I don't have an appointment."

"He takes walk-ins," said the man with the wrapped hand.

Sabrina looked at me like she recognized me but didn't know from where.

"I'm a friend of Ruth's. I stopped by your rehearsal yesterday afternoon." I didn't bother to say that I'd seen her at the restaurant. I didn't want to embarrass her.

"Oh," she said.

I held out my hand. "I'm Willy Boden."

She took it and gave me a quick shake. "Sabrina Miller." She cast a sideways glance at the teenage boy. "My son Josh." She patted his shoulder. "He has growing pains."

"Don't we all," I told her.

The kid, whose hair was darker than his mom's but just as curly, glanced at me before rolling his eyes and returning his attention to his cell phone.

I took the empty spot on the other side of the reader and addressed Sabrina. "Tragic what happened to Evelyn Meyers, huh?" Every eye in the room pinned me. "I'm not trying to be indelicate. I found the body, and I'm still a little shook up," I lied. Sabrina had been pretty desperate yesterday, and I was curious as to how far she might have gone to alleviate that desperation.

The woman with the black hair said, "You found her?"

"Yes. It was awful."

"Evelyn had her share of problems. Most of them her own creation."

"It sounds like you knew her pretty well."

"As well as anyone could know her, I suppose."

The door next to the counter opened. Billy Bob Smith, all six and a half feet of him, poked his head through and said, "Come on back, Nicole."

The woman put her tablet in a pink satchel next to her feet. "I'm Evelyn's niece. You know my mom and dad, Sid and Jean Taylor. He told me about you last night." She smiled. "Nothing bad. No worries."

Doctor Smith looked at me. "Chavvah called. I'll see you but after my patients. Okay?"

Since I didn't have any choice, I said, "Okay." I hoped it wouldn't be too long. I really wanted to shower and have a little time to work on my hair before my dinner date with Brady. The humidity had turned my copper curls into copper wire.

"She was a hateful woman," Sabrina said after Nicole and Doctor Smith left.

Her son put in his earbuds. Teenagers. He might not want to hear what his mother had to say, but I did. "I haven't heard much good about her since all this happened."

Sabrina wrung her hands. "And you won't. Evelyn Meyers didn't care about anyone but Evelyn Meyers."

"I don't mean to pry," I said, even though I really did. "What did Evelyn do to you?"

"Nothing." Sabrina sighed. "I did it to myself. When Josh's dad left, I could barely afford the rent on a jewelry store clerk's salary and put groceries on the table. I've had some extra bills lately, and it's put me way behind."

The teenager abruptly stood up. "Jesus, Mom. I'll wait outside. Come get me when Doc is ready to see me." He stomped out of the waiting area.

"He's been like that for two years. It would have been different if Clay had died, but the bastard left us to start a new life somewhere else. He barely sees Josh anymore. It takes its toll."

Hearing your mom talk about all your dirty laundry in a public setting probably took its toll as well. I didn't fault Sabrina, though. Raising a child with someone would be difficult enough, and if I'd had to do it on my own, I'd probably drown in anxiety.

Like Brady had after his wife disappeared.

I nodded sagely. "He'll probably grow out of it."

"Will he?" she asked hopefully.

I had no idea. "Sure." What the fuck did I know? I'd been single for my entire thirty-three years. "Are you enjoying the play? I've always been interested in acting." Kind of like I was doing right now.

"It's been...stressful. Evelyn made it hard to enjoy. I guess now that she's gone I'll take over the role of Gertrude."

"Yeah? How come?"

"I was Evelyn's understudy. You know how theater is."

I really didn't. "Sure. What part were you playing before?"

"I was a handmaiden. A pretty small role. No lines."

"Where you at rehearsal last night?"

"Yes, but..." She rubbed her hands on her slacks. "I..." The door opened again.

The doc stuck his head out. "Where's Josh?"

"I'll get him." Sabrina leaped to her feet and pounded on the front door. Josh, apparently familiar with that method of communication, jerked the door open and sauntered in looking surlier than when he left. Sabrina gazed at me. "It was nice talking to you, Willy."

"Maybe we can do it again sometime," I said.

She smiled. "I'd really like that." Josh had already followed Doc Smith to the back.

I stood and went to the counter, scribbled my name and number on the bottom corner of the sign-in sheet, and ripped it off. I handed it to Sabrina. "Give me a call sometime."

She placed the number in her purse. "I better get inside. Josh will deny all problems if I'm not there."

I gave her a sympathetic smile. "Boys can be difficult." At least the ones I've dated in the past had been.

After she went inside, the man with the wrapped hand stared at me. "You're not from around here, are you?"

"Nope." But I wanted to be. "I'm just in town for a visit."

"I'm Elton Brown," he said. "I own the furniture store downtown." He held up his hand. "Cut myself on a band saw this afternoon. I make furniture to order." With his free hand, he grabbed his wallet from his back pocket and took a card from it. He held it out. "If you decide to stick around, give me a call. I have a way of matching wood to a person, and I just got in a large hunk of black walnut that has you written all over it."

"Uhm, thanks." I took the card. "I'll let you know."

He put his wallet back. "I'm the gravedigger, by the way."

Was that some kind of euphemism? A veiled threat? I didn't say anything, because, what was there to say when a guy tells you he digs graves? The furniture maker added, "In the play. I'm the gravedigger. You know, the guy who finds Yorick's skull."

Oh, Hamlet. Duh. I started to ask him about rehearsal last night, but Doctor Smith picked that moment to open the door. He held it for Nicole Taylor who'd been trailing right behind him. The dark-haired beauty held a small bottle of pills. "Thanks, Doc. I'll let you know if these help her anxiety."

"You're welcome." Billy Bob Smith gave her a warm smile, his soft gray hair framing his wide cheeks. Damn, Chavvah was a lucky gal. "It's nice to have you back home. Tell Jean she should come in next time though." He shifted his attention to Elton. "You're up. Let's get that hand taken care of." Almost as an afterthought, he cast his silver gaze on me. "Still here, huh?"

"Yep. Still here."

He sighed. "It might be another half hour."

"I can wait." A half hour had already passed so it would be four-thirty before I talked to the doctor. Maybe another half hour before I got on the road to Ruth's. Damn it. I wondered how Brady felt about women in hats.

CHAPTER NINE

*E*very ticking second spanned an eternity. At one point, I started to think the doc was torturing me on purpose. Like he knew I had important plans and was determined to make me late, so when he finally discharged Josh Miller and Elton Brown, I heaved a relieved sigh.

The tall lycanthrope led me back to his office. Paperwork cluttered the desk. His filing system was non-existent. "I know you want to see Evelyn Meyer's autopsy report, Ms. Boden, but I can't share information from an ongoing investigation."

"Doctor Smith," I said.

"Call me, Billy Bob."

"Fine, if you call me Willy."

"It's a strange name for a girl."

I laughed. "You're one to talk."

"Billy Bob is a perfectly fine name for a man."

"But strange for a doctor. It doesn't exactly scream 'I have an advanced degree.'"

"I get that a lot." He shook his head. "Like I said, Willy, I can't share information with you, no matter how much it might irritate my mate."

"I'm afraid it's official business now. You can call the Tri-State Council office if you want to verify, but President Stenson himself has asked me to investigate independently of the sheriff's office."

Billy Bob narrowed his gaze on me. "Why would he do that? Did you say something to him to make him think Sheriff Taylor couldn't handle it because that man has over twenty years of experience in law enforcement--"

I held up my hand. "I didn't diminish Sid in any way. I barely even mentioned him in my report. Evelyn Meyers was on Stenson's radar, and for reasons he didn't make clear to me, he wants me to look into her death. I do what I'm told."

"I've heard that about you."

Wait. No doubt Chavvah and Billy Bob knew about Sunny's abilities. I was stunned that a town this size could keep a secret that big. "You know about Sunny?"

"Sunny knew about you." He thinned his lips in a frown. "Weeks ago. Are you going to tell the council about her?"

"What did Sunny say?"

"You can be trusted."

"And what do you say?"

"The jury is still out."

"Fair enough, Billy Bob." I didn't want to bring pain to anyone in Peculiar. "So, what can you tell me about Evelyn's death?"

"Well, she didn't die from exsanguination. I believed getting stabbed with the foil occurred after death or close to it. There was very little blood loss, and when she arrived here, livor mortis was already apparent."

I wasn't a forensics expert, but I knew livor mortis meant Evelyn had been supine after she died. When lying face-up in a horizontal position, blood pools in the body's tissues causing a purplish-red discoloration. "How long does it take for livor mortis to occur?"

"It's not observable until at least two hours after death."

"When did she get here?"

"I didn't get to the crime scene until nearly nine o'clock. By the time the coroner Mark Smart and I were able to remove Evelyn from the wall without damaging the evidence and get her back to the clinic, it was nearly ten-thirty."

So, if livor mortis was present, it proved she was on her backside for more than a few minutes before she was moved, so she had to have been killed closer to six-thirty than eight-thirty. "Was there any bruising on her heels?"

He shook his head. "It doesn't appear as if she were dragged. She would have been lifted to the spot behind the curtains."

Therianthropes had more strength than the average person, but we weren't superhuman strong, not in our hominid forms. It would have taken someone extremely strong and coordinated to have pinned Evelyn against the wall without help and without leaving any obvious trace behind. "Was blood found anywhere else? I smelled it when I got close to the victim, but not before."

"Not that I know of, but Sheriff Taylor could better answer that question."

"Any petechial hemorrhaging in the eyes?"

"Yes, but no marks on her neck to indicate strangulation and her hyoid bone was intact."

Her throat would've been crushed if a shifter had strangled her. But petechial hemorrhaging meant she was denied oxygen for long enough that the capillary veins in her eyes burst. "So, was she smothered?"

"I can't rule it out yet."

"Damn, so no concrete COD, huh?"

"Not yet." He leaned back in his chair. "I sent a tox screen to a lab in Kansas City, but the results won't be in for several days." He looked at me. "I might have one theory, though. Do you want to see the body?"

I tried not to sound too eager when I answered. "Hell, yes."

EVELYN'S BODY was in the surgery room on a metal table. A white sheet covered her from her chest to her knees. I put on gloves I grabbed from a dispenser. Gently, I turned over her hands. I wasn't squeamish, but touching dead flesh was not a Saturday night at the disco. There were scabby scrapes on her palms.

"I witnessed Evelyn fall yesterday on the sidewalk. The

scrapes could have happened then. They seem to be healing."

"Can I see the livor mortis?" Maybe the distribution of mottling might tell me something.

"Sure." He moved to the opposite side of the table and rolled the corpse onto its side.

Purple patterns painted Evelyn's buttocks and back. She had a puncture wound where her flesh had been pushed out by the sword below the left ribs.

"Okay, Doc. You have a lot field experience. I've seen your records." He'd been a military medic before becoming a doctor, and he'd worked in forensics for a while before relocating to Peculiar. "Give me your best guess."

"See how bright pink her skin is, even a day after death?"

"Yes."

He walked over to the refrigerator and took out a small vile of blood. "Her skin color and blood vibrancy makes me think it might be cyanide or carbon monoxide poisoning, but I don't want to jump to conclusions."

"How would someone even get access to cyanide?"

Billy Bob shrugged. "It wouldn't be easy. It's used in gold mining processes, but there's nothing like that around Peculiar or even in Missouri as far as I know."

"I guess it's a wait and see thing then." At least I could mostly rule Jo Jo out. Where in the world would that kid get cyanide?

"I'm afraid so."

"It wouldn't take much cyanide to kill her in a couple hours. A large dose would have done it in minutes. But how would they have dosed her without her suspecting? You don't take drinks from people you don't know."

"Unless you're at a public establishment, like a restaurant."

"She was at Sunny's Outlook for lunch. You think your soon to be sister-in-law is a poisoner?"

"I hope your teasing."

"I am," I admitted. Sunny wasn't on my suspect list at all. "Whoever offed her was pissed enough or calculated enough to pin her to the wall with the sword after. Probably hoping to throw us off the scent of the actual cause of death."

Billy Bob shrugged. "I can't commit to COD yet, but that's as good as any hypothesis."

"Hello," I heard Chavvah holler from out in the hall. "Doc, you back there?"

I watched the way Billy Bob's posture perked up at the sound of his mate's voice.

"In here," he said.

"Congrats on the upcoming wedding," I offered. "Did you get the wedding venue?"

"Yes, we did," said Chav as she breezed into the room. She flung her arms around Billy Bob's neck, and they shared an intimate kiss. Then she noticed the body. Her face paled. "Are you both about done in here?"

"Yep," Billy Bob said. "Unless Willy has any more questions."

Chav looked at the clock on the wall. "It's after five o'clock, Willy. Don't you have a date tonight?"

"Shit, yes." I turned to leave. "Thanks for your help, Billy Bob. Let me know if the tests come back conclusive."

"You got it," I heard him say as I bolted from the clinic.

CHAPTER TEN

"**O**h my God, I smell like ass, and my hair looks like I stuck a wet finger in a light socket." I hadn't brought down any good date clothes, so Dakota had lent me a bright blue strappy summer dress. The hem hit me just above the knee. Michele and I wore the same size shoe, so the girl had given me a pair of cute sandals with red, blue, pink, and yellow flowers across the strap over the toes.

"You don't smell like a butt," Ruth assured me. "And your hair is charming." Though the way she was fussing over it with hairspray and pressing it down told me she thought it anything but charming. "Besides, Brady doesn't care about your hair."

"Doesn't he?" I asked panicked, my voice raising an octave in the process. "Doesn't he? I don't have a lot going for me, woman. My hair, when right, is an asset, but when wrong, is a frizzy liability. I mean, I'm short, I have a gazillion freckles on my face. Brady is going to race away from the curb if I go out there looking like Medusa's ugly sister."

"You don't look like anyone's ugly sister."

"Great! I'm an ugly-only-child then." I slumped down in the chair in front of Dakota's vanity. "I am losing my mind. I've had dates before. Lots of them. I am usually confident. What is happening to me?"

Ruth, still trying to tame my curls, giggled. "It's different when you care."

"What's that supposed to mean?" I blotted at my mascara where I'd blinked it onto my cheek.

"Who was the last man you went on a date with?"

Since Halloween, I hadn't accepted a single date offer. "Jesse Jessop, a fox from Platte City. He had some council business. One thing led to another."

"Really?"

"Not that," I said quickly. "I just mean, he flirted, I flirted, he asked me out, I said yes. It was a simple dinner and movie then home. There wasn't much spark there." Which pretty much summed up every guy I'd met since the first time I saw Brady. Gah!

"Were you worried how the date would turn out?"

"No."

"Did you care if your hair was a little frizzy or your freckles too prominent?"

"No."

"Did you worry whether he would even like you?"

"Of course not."

"Why?"

I crossed my arms over my chest. "Fine. I see your point. What am I supposed to do? I can't care less."

"Of course not. You're just going to have to live through it like the rest of us mortals who have gone before you. You'll survive your date with Brady, and if he doesn't like you because your hair's a little wild, then he isn't the right man for you anyway."

"Tell me about you and Ed. When did you start dating?"

Ruth put down the spray and placed her hands on my shoulders. "Ed was a year ahead of me. We both grew up in Peculiar. My folks live over on the north side of town, and Ed's parents have a place out in the country. We were both deer therians, but as you know, that doesn't always mean two people are going to match up, just because their animals are the same. Brady and Ed were friends. The best of, actually. And stupid me, I kind of had a crush on Brady. I mean, even at fourteen years of age, he had a fire in him the drew everyone to his warmth. I went to the junior high spring fling with every intent on asking Brady to dance with me, but when I walked in, *Time of My Life* from the movie *Dirty Dancing* blared from the speakers, and Ed came right up to me and said, "Ruth Smalley, would you like to dance with me? I could see his boldness cost him. There was a strain behind his smoky brown eyes as he waited for my answer." Ruth paused, caught up in the memory.

"And?" I prompted.

"I said yes, of course. He was so light on his feet, and I hadn't realized how muscled he was until I had my hands on his arms. Halfway through the song, I thought, damn, I really like this boy. Then my palms began to sweat, and my heart raced. Did my hair look okay? Was my deodorant holding up? Was my dress pretty enough? Was I pretty enough?"

I'd leaned forward with anticipation. "Then what?"

"Ed leaned down to my ear and said, 'I can't believe I'm dancing with the most beautiful girl in town.'"

My eyes widened, my own heart racing for the young girl at the birth of romance. "What did you say?"

"Nothing!" Ruth laughed. "He'd made me shy. He'd made me care. So, I let my body language do the talking. I stepped in closer to him, our bodies touching for the first time since the dance started. Mr. Piers, my seventh grade English teacher, came up and stuck a hand between us and told us not to make him break out a ruler."

"To beat you?"

"Yes, to beat us," Ruth agreed sarcastically. "Crickets on toast, where the heck were you raised? The ruler was to measure the distance between us. There was a three-inch rule in place for school dances. *Dirty Dancing*, even a decade later, had all the adults nervous."

"Well, Swayze was a sexy beast."

"No lie." Ruth picked at a loose thread on her dark green blouse. "Anyways, I never had eyes for anyone but Ed after that, and it was the same for him. We got married shortly after Ed's high school graduation." She laughed. "I started my senior year a married woman. My parents had a fit, as you can imagine."

I dabbed on some cream blush. "Wow, I've never been

with a guy longer than three months, I can't imagine being with someone for more than two decades."

Ruth got up and stood behind me. She placed her hands on my shoulders and met my gaze through the mirror. "I think you can. I think you're imagining it already. And that's what scares you the most."

"Maybe Sunny's not the only psychic in town."

Ruth's mouth formed a small "o." "She told you?"

I patted her hand. "Yes. And don't worry, I'm not mad at you. It wasn't your secret to share."

"Mr. Corman's here!" Emma Ray, one of Ruth's younger daughters, shouted. "He just pulled up!"

My pulse quickened. I grabbed Ruth's hand. "He hasn't been with anyone except Rose Ann. How am I supposed to compete with that?"

"Rose Ann is dead, honey. There is no competition."

"I'm awful to men. I've been told I'm a maneater. I don't want to hurt Brady. God, what if I hurt him? You go downstairs and tell him I'm sick or something."

"First, you're not one of my children, and even if you were, I wouldn't make an excuse for you. Second, the fact that you're worried you're going to hurt Brady, probably means you won't. So, get your cute little heinie up and go see a man about a dinner."

"You are one tough chick, Ruth."

She urged me up from the chair. "It takes one to know one."

In the kitchen, Brady and Ed leaned against the counter, drinking coffee and discussing the weather. In Ruth's story, they'd been best friends. Now, they seemed amiable enough, but I felt a distance between them.

I couldn't keep my eyes off Brady. Christ, that man knew how to fill out a pair of jeans. The cut showed off his popping bootie and his muscular thighs. He wore a blue button down western shirt that stretched across his wide chest, and the short sleeves gave me a free ticket to the gun show. I could do chin-ups on those steel biceps. His look was finished off with a pair of mahogany cowboy boots.

When he saw me, his amber eyes lit with pleasure. His Adam's apple worked up and down as he closed the distance to me. "You look real pretty," he said.

My I.Q. dropped a hundred points. "You clean up good, too." Doh.

"You both look handsome," Ruth said. "If it's not too late, you should come back for some pie and coffee after dinner, Brady. We'd love to have you."

Brady glanced at Ed. He nodded. "You should," Ed said. "If it's not too late." He gave Brady a wink, and I swear my hunky coyote shifter blushed.

"Sure," he said. He glanced down at me. "You ready to go?"

There was a knock at the front door. Emma Ray ran to the window. "Michele! It's Roger!"

"Be right there," Michele shouted. I guess I wasn't the only one in the house with a date. I didn't know much about the kid, but the way Brady scowled when he heard Roger's name, I was instantly ready to not like the boy.

Roger came inside and stood by the door as we passed

him. He wore a ball cap that shadowed his face, but I could see his dark hair sprouting out around the rim. He was built well and had an aura of danger—a real rebel without a clue vibe. Outside, Brady walked me down to his truck parked at the curb. Right behind his truck was a black car with tinted windows. I recognized it immediately.

"That's the car that tried to run down Evelyn."

"You sure?"

I walked around the front to get a closer look at the license plate. ERG was the first three letters. Definitely the vehicle. "Yes, I'm sure. We should call the sheriff."

Michele and Roger, hand-in-hand, walked out of the house. She was giggling about something until Roger shouted, "Hey, what are you doing to my car?"

I stared at the teenager. "This is yours?"

"Yeah. So what?"

"You need to come down to the police station and answer a few questions."

"About what?"

"About why you tried to run Evelyn Meyers down yesterday in front of Dolly's Beauty shop."

"You're crazy, lady."

Michele freed her hand from Roger's. "What's Willy talking about Roger? You said you were working yesterday."

"I was."

"Working on murder," I muttered.

"I didn't have nothing do with that old bitch's death," Roger said. He had his keys out and was moving toward the car. "And I ain't talking to the cops about nothing."

Brady snarled, but before he could act, I'd already placed myself between Roger and the vehicle. "We can do this the easy way or the hard way."

"Or we can do nothing at all." He reached out to shove me aside. I used his own forward movement as a counter-balance and slammed him face first into the lawn.

Michele let out a jerking sob as I twisted his hand and forearm behind his back and shoved my knee into his spine. "Hard way it is." I looked up at Brady who had an unreadable expression on his face. I grimaced. "Sorry about ruining our date. Can you call nine-one-one?"

CHAPTER ELEVEN

*D*eputy **Farraday arrived** at Ruth's to take Roger into custody. At this point, he was only a person of interest, but it didn't mean he killed Evelyn Meyers. Which is what I told a hysterical Michele who'd insisted on riding down to the police station with Brady and me.

The unhappy girl shot daggers at me the whole way there. "I saw what I saw, Michele. I'm not going to lie about it."

"But you didn't have to humiliate him," she said.

My mood soured even more. "He didn't have to try and shove me."

"That's your excuse?" she snapped. "He started it? And my mom says I'm immature."

I was so not having this lose-lose conversation. Brady had been strangely quiet. "Are you mad at me too?"

My question startled him from his reverie. "No. I'm

disappointed about dinner, but I'm not mad. Roger Parks is a punk."

"He is not," Michele protested from the back seat.

I rolled my eyes. I was more inclined to agree with Brady. If Roger had nothing to hide, then he should've come with us to talk to the police. He didn't have to try to get all macho with me.

"You're awfully quiet," I said to Brady.

His brow was furrowed, creating lines in his forehead. "Just thinking."

"I wish you'd tell me what you're thinking about." Like, was he thinking, man, this Willy chick is a psycho? What have I gotten myself into and how soon can I find the exit?

I might have been pondering all of the above if Brady had taken someone down right before our date. I was so blowing this between Brady and me, and not in a fun way.

"I can't right now." He glanced in the rearview mirror at Michele. "You understand, right?"

"Sure." I tugged my lower lip between my teeth then let it go.

Brady quietly groaned in a way that made my thighs quiver.

I touched his knee. "You'll let me make tonight up to you? Maybe dinner tomorrow night?"

He adjusted his position in the seat. "Tonight's not over yet."

Hubba hubba. Rawr.

Sheriff Taylor was in his office, working late hours, I assumed. There was no such thing as time off during a murder investigation. I needed to let him know about my orders from Stenson. Sid deserved to know that I would be conducting my own inquiries. I had worked with the sheriff's department last June on the serial killer case, but this death was more personal for Sheriff Taylor, and there was little doubt the culprit was a local as well. I feared he would take my news as interference, or worse, he might see me as a usurper.

"I'll be back in a minute," I told Brady. "Can you stay with Michele?" More quietly, I added, "I'm worried she'll throw herself on Roger to protect the little asshole."

Brady shook his head but smiled. "I'm on the job."

I rapped on the Sheriff's door.

"Come in," he said.

I opened the door. His eyes were bloodshot, his skin dull.

"Hey, Sid, can I talk to you for a minute?"

He waved me in. "Come inside, Willy. You can close the door behind you."

I took a seat in the chair opposite his desk. I'd never been good at easing into a conversation, so I shot straight from the hip. "I mentioned Evelyn's murder to President Stenson, and he's asked me to get involved. I don't want to step on your toes. I'm hoping we can work together on this."

Sid slid his chair back and steepled his fingers. His gray and black eyebrows squished together and apart as he studied me. I didn't flinch. It wasn't the first time I'd been placed in the hot seat, and I was certain it wouldn't be the last.

"I don't like the Tri-State Council poking its nose in town business."

"I understand your feelings. I'd be upset if outside law enforcement tried to hound in on one of my investigations. However, I'm here, and I'm willing to help."

"Would you like some coffee?" He stood up and topped off his cup from a pot on a small stand in the corner of his cramped office.

"No, thanks. I try to limit my caffeine to early mornings. Just enough to peel my eyes open." Unless I was on a stakeout. Otherwise, too much caffeine during the day gave me the jitters.

He turned back around and peered at me with his stormy gray eyes. "If the council wants you to investigate, I won't stand in your way."

"Will you give me access to your investigation?"

He glowered. "Yes."

"This could be a good thing, Sid. Maybe you should take a step back. It's hard to be objective investigating the death of a loved one."

"You didn't have a problem investigating when Jerry Blackwell was killed last June."

I had dated Jerry for a couple of months before the Jubilee and his horrifying death. We'd fought the day before his body was found behind Sunny's Outlook. He'd been skinned alive, his eyes taken in the process. I shuddered. "True, but I didn't love Jerry." Hell, I'd barely felt his loss at all, which probably made me a terrible person.

"I didn't love Evelyn."

"She's your sister-in-law."

"I can be objective, Willy." He sat down and scooted back up to his desk. "Thank you for the courtesy call. Farraday can give you access to Evelyn Meyers files."

I knew a dismissal when I heard it. "Did you all find anything of interest at her home? Anything suspicious?"

Sheriff Taylor shook his head. "Nope."

Had he looked at her bank records? His short answer told me he was done talking. Besides, I could read about anything they found in the documentation. I left Sid's office and walked out into the main staging area just as Tyler Thompson came into the room from the back. He finished tucking in his uniform shirt. I heard a toilet flushing down the hall. He looked at me then at Brady with a curious expression. Then he saw his sister. "What are you doing here?"

Michele burst into tears. Brady groaned. I shuffled uncomfortably and headed over to Farraday.

"And...and..." I heard Michele say, along with a series of hiccups, "she beat him up and had him arrested!"

"She didn't beat me up," Roger complained.

"Quiet, you," Tyler ordered the young man.

"And he's not arrested," I said. "He's just being questioned. And the only reason I took him down--" Michele turned her face into her brother's chest and ignored me. "Never mind." I placed my palm down in front of Roger. "Why'd you try to run Evelyn down?"

"I didn't," the boy denied. "I..." He glanced at Michele and back to me. "I was working."

"Uh huh." I tisked. "What kind of work do you do?"

He scooted down in his chair. "This and that."

"This and that must be very profitable," I said. "Those are one-hundred and fifty-dollar jeans, your shoes are at least a hundred dollars..." I whistled. "And that sweet ride." I shook my head. "I'm thinking I need to change professions. What kind of experience do you need for a job in this and that?"

"You're a real bitch."

"And you're a real gentlemen," I shot back. How could Michele see anything good in this guy?

"Apparently, you need a broader vocabulary," added Eldin.

Roger glared at him. "I want a lawyer." He crossed his arms as if he'd won some small victory. "I'm not saying another word until I speak to a lawyer."

"Do you have a lawyer?" Eldin asked.

Roger's face reddened. "I know my rights."

"Someone has spent a little too much time watching *Law & Order*." I flicked the back of Roger's head. "You aren't under arrest, asshole. Besides," I looked at Eldin, "do you guys even have lawyers in Peculiar?"

"Not since Neville Lutjen."

"That's not strictly true," Brady said. "I'm still licensed in the state of Missouri. But I specialized in tax law, not criminal."

My mouth dropped open. I used the back of my hand to close it. "I thought you were a handyman."

"I'm handy, too."

"I don't want Mr. Corman as my lawyer." Roger turned his back to Brady. That's when I noticed a cut in his hairline by his right temple, and a bruise colored his right cheek.

"You get in a fight with Evelyn Meyers when you killed her?" I pressed my fingertip into the bruise. "Did she fight back?"

"I didn't kill her," he said again.

"How did you manage to stage the body? You had her pinned up like a prom dress."

"Leave him alone," Michele cried.

Sheriff Taylor stepped out of his office. "Thompson, take your sister home."

"No," the moon-eyed teenager protested. "I'm not leaving him. Roger!" she shouted as Tyler backed her toward the exit. "Roger!"

The boy moaned and slumped down even more.

Once the front door closed behind Tyler and Michele, Roger's whole demeanor changed. "If I tell you the truth, will you keep it just between us? Michele can't know."

I tapped the desk in front of Roger. "Kid, if you killed Ms. Meyers, everyone's going to know."

"I didn't...Gah!" He threw up his hands. "I was with Karina Wells yesterday afternoon. She's the one who almost ran over Ms. Meyers."

"You better explain," Eldin said.

"I broke it off with Karina a month ago. She called me yesterday morning and told me she had to talk to me. Now, I don't want to mess up anything with Michele, so I tell her, no, but then Karina says she's pregnant, and I'm like, bullshit. She tells me that if I don't meet her in the afternoon, she's going to tell Michele that I'm still sleeping with her, which is a fucking lie."

"You really do need to broaden your vocabulary," I said. "Go on."

"Anyway, I agree to meet with her at Coyote Creek."

I looked at Brady. "It's a park on the west side of town just after the road dead ends. It has some picnic areas and hiking trails," he explained.

"Cool." I focused back on Roger. "Then what?"

"The bit—er, Karina told me she wasn't pregnant, she just wanted to see me. I told her to piss off. She grabbed my car keys and jumped into the driver seat. I got in the passenger side when she started it up. She drove like a maniac all the way through town hoping someone would see us together and tell Michele, but it was a waste of time because my windows are tinted darker than factory spec."

"You need to remove the tint on the front door windows and the windshield," Eldin said. "As it is, you are looking at a fine."

"So, you believe me?" The color began to return to his face as a trickle of sweat slid down in front of his ear.

"Why did Karina jump the curb at Evelyn?"

Roger scowled. "That was my fault. I was trying to get her to pull over. She let go of the wheel when I jerked it my way, and the car went out of control. You can see why I don't want Michele to find out."

"Look, fella, I'm not a priest, and this isn't confession. I get that you are worried your girl is going to see you as a lying scumbag, but I can't guarantee what you say won't come out in the course of the investigation." I walked around to the other side of him. "Where were you between six-thirty and eight-thirty?"

"I took Michele home from rehearsal, and I ran a few errands."

"Can anyone vouch for your whereabouts?" Eldin asked.

The kid moved his gaze from Eldin to me and then to Brady. He sighed. "No."

I touched his bruise again. "Who knocked you around?"

Roger tried to swat my hand away, but I moved it away before he made contact. "Too slow," I told him. "I'm going to ask you again, who did you have a fight with?"

"I ran into a door," he said. The set of his jaw told me I wouldn't get any more information from Roger.

I nodded to Eldin. "Thanks for letting me play in your sandbox."

The deputy smiled. "I'll be Lacey to your Cagney anytime, Willy."

Brady's hand wrapped my upper arm. He leaned down and said, "Can I talk to you privately?"

My belly got jittery under his hard stare. What had I done wrong? "I...okay."

Eldin jerked his thumb behind toward the back. "Breakroom's at the back of the hall."

Brady took my hand and practically dragged me back to the room. He closed the door behind us.

"I'm really sorry if I did something--"

He shut me up with a kiss that made my knees wobble and my thighs quake. I wrapped my hands behind his neck to keep myself off the floor. His warm lips parted over mine, his tongue sweeping my tonsils, and hot damn, I thought I would faint as elation overwhelmed me. He finally eased back, his kissing growing softer, gentler until we were staring into each other's eyes like horny teenagers.

He pressed his forehead to mine. "Wow," he said, his throat hoarse with lust. "I never knew a game of good cop bad cop could be so sexy."

I smirked. "I have handcuffs and a nightstick if you want an encore."

A knock on the door parted us. Eldin asked, "Do you have any more questions for Roger?"

"No," I told him. "Not right now." I had a lot more investigating to do. Every answer created more questions.

"Okay. I'm letting him go for now then."

"Sounds good." I raised my brows at Brady who was still giving me the "I'm gonna rock your world stare."

He took my hand and brought my fingers to his lips. "I think we can still make dinner."

My stomach growled. "I could eat, and then maybe after we could..."

"Go to Ruth's for pie?"

I guess we were still taking it slow, but damn, every bit of me wanted to be touching every bit of him. I hid my disappointment with a smile. "Sounds perfect."

CHAPTER TWELVE

*T*he next morning, I awoke at eight-fifty with a kink in my neck and an ache in my chest. Brady had given me a sweet kiss when I'd walked him out to his truck, but it had lacked the intensity of our break room make-out. I crawled out of bed and headed down the hall to the bathroom. The door was unlocked. Sleepily, I pushed it open.

"Hey!" Leroy shouted, dropping a comic book over his lap.

"Shit, sorry." I closed the door. I'd lived by myself for so long it hadn't occurred to me I'd walk in on someone on the pot. Leroy was Emma Ray's twin, which meant he was seventeen. I raced back to Dakota's room, praying I hadn't scarred the boy for life. Hans would have needed therapy if a stranger walked in on him pooping.

Ten minutes later, Ruth knocked on my door. "Coast is clear," she said. "Leroy took off with some friends."

I opened the door. "I'm so sorry! I woke up late and forgot about the schedule."

"After eight the bathrooms are all fair game. First come, first serve." She gave me a sympathetic smile. "Don't worry about Leroy. He lives in a house full of girls, and that's not the first time he's been walked in on. That'll teach the boy to lock the door next time."

"Are you sure the coast is clear? I really have to pee."

"It's all yours." Ruth walked to the bedroom window.

Sunrays bathed her face in a way that made her look as if she were caught in an Instagram filter that highlighted her dainty femininity. Ruth was as pretty on the inside as she was on the out. I'd never had a friend quite like her. Most of the women I hung with were real ball-busters. I loved them, but they were blunt as hell with the way they talked. Hell, with the way they lived their lives. Ruth was subtle, more mom-like, but just as honest.

She propped herself against the windowsill. "It's nice to see Brady happy." She paused and then looked like she wanted to say more. Instead, she shook her head. "I'll leave you to it. I have coffee and cinnamon rolls downstairs."

I smiled. "Best bed and breakfast ever."

She chuckled, but I could tell her heart wasn't in it. "Ruth, is everything okay?"

"Do you really think Roger Parks had anything to do with Evelyn's murder?"

I answered honestly. "I don't know. Maybe. He's hiding something. I just don't know what."

"I'm afraid for Michele." She nibbled at the side of her thumbnail. "I never liked the boy, but I didn't think he was dangerous, not really. Besides, I learned long ago that I can't choose who my children want to love. And while I didn't think things would last between her and Roger, I worry that she'll somehow romanticize what happened last night. That it will make her want him more." Ruth sighed, the worry creasing her brow. "Michele, out of all my kids, has a wild streak in her, especially when it comes to the opposite sex. Especially bad boys."

I snorted and immediately regretted it as Ruth cast me a look of disapproval. "Sorry. It's just that I understand Michele far better than I want to. When I was her age, I was Michele. Really, up until last year. Inappropriate men were my thing." The fact that I was crazy for a man who might be emotionally unavailable told me it might still be my thing. "I can't tell you not to worry, but Michele is a smart girl. I have a feeling she'll make the right decision when it comes to Roger Parks." Especially if she accidentally found out about his rendezvous with a certain ex-girlfriend. Just sayin'.

"You think so?" The same features that made her look delicate, also made her look vulnerable.

"I know so." I stood up and gave her a hug, my bladder complaining the entire time. I pressed my thighs together. "Now, I really need to use the bathroom."

NEAR NOON, I headed to the Sheriff's Department. I wanted to look over their notes and evidence to see if it might add to anything I'd uncovered about Evelyn's death, which frankly wasn't much. It was hard trying to solve a crime where half the town were suspects. I needed to nail down alibis to eliminate the most obvious people.

Michael Connelly was working with Tyler Thompson. The sheriff was conspicuously absent.

I gave Deputy Thompson a nod. "Afternoon. Didn't you work last night?"

"Only a half shift. We're short of staff these days, but more hours mean more money."

"Oh, yeah?"

He grinned. "My wife Darla is pregnant again."

"Congratulations." I clapped him on the back. "That's great news." I looked around for an empty desk. "Did the sheriff let you know I'd be helping with the investigation?"

"Yes. He said to give you anything you needed."

"I hope you all don't think I'm overstepping."

"Frankly, I'm exhausted," Tyler said. "I don't mind the extra set of hands."

"Me either," said Connelly. "We used to have a few more deputies, but after the skinnings last year, a few of them quit to seek other employment. I considered it myself, actually, but when there aren't any serial killers running loose, Peculiar is a pretty easy town to police."

"Is there an empty desk I can use for now?"

"Take that one over there." Tyler pointed at an empty one near the wall. "It hasn't been occupied for a while. If you need a computer, you can use mine."

"Right now, I just need the files. I'd really like to see where you all are at and go from there."

"You got it." Connelly grabbed a shallow box from his

desk and put it on the one they'd given me. "Eldin put it all together. He said you might be coming in today."

"He's a righteous cop," I said.

Connelly smiled. "Yeah, good dude."

The first thing I looked at was the report of Evelyn's house. It was sparse. The notes indicated there was nothing in the home to suggest the murder took place there. And there was no obvious evidence found to indicate a motive or suspect. I guess the bank ledger wasn't suspicious to anyone but me. I saw Connelly's name on the report.

"Michael, did you participate in the search of the Meyers' house?"

"Yes."

"Did you guys find anything out of the ordinary? Nothing is noted in the report."

"No. Just basic office stuff." He shrugged. "Why?"

Because I found a ledger indicating Evelyn Meyers was worth a small fortune when I illegally searched her place before you. Thanks to Sunny. The Peculiar police were playing nice with me, and I didn't want to jeopardize my relationship with them by admitting what I'd done. "No reason." I sighed. Well, fuck me.

I moved on to the crime scene notes next. There had been a small amount of blood on the stage a few feet from where the body had been placed. Was that where she'd been stabbed? I rummaged through the pictures. Eldin had done a thorough job of documenting the scene, but I didn't see anything new that I hadn't already seen watching the video I took.

They had interviewed the entire cast of the play, but no crew. There wasn't a statement from Brady or from Taylor Thompson. I read over Sabrina's account. She said she hadn't spoken to Evelyn during rehearsal and after, she picked her son up from a friend's house. The friend's parents corroborated that she had picked up Josh at six-forty-five. They noted the time because they were getting ready to go out to dinner.

Did Sabrina have an alibi after all?

Milo Greene, who'd agreed to talk to me at three today, had said he'd left and went straight home. He hadn't seen Evelyn again after that. His wife didn't get home from her parents until after eight, so he had no alibi for the time in between rehearsal and eight p.m.

Sunny had gone to the courthouse. Her and Babe had gone home together to relieve the babysitter. After Ruth phoned Sunny for the community center key, she came back into town early. Alibi.

Eldin Farraday went home to shower, and only returned to town after the sheriff called him to help work the crime scene. No alibi.

Roger Parks said he took Michele home and ran errands after, but no one saw him to corroborate his statement. Freaking punk. No alibi.

Michele went home to babysit Linus since her dad worked late and her mom was having a girl's night. Alibi.

Billy Bob, who was apparently playing the ghost, had skipped rehearsals because of a house call. Patient backed his account. Alibi.

Oh, and this was interesting, and it added to the timeline. Evelyn had called Bob Winston, the manager of the community center, demanding that he let her into the community center to retrieve her fruit. He said, she hadn't made a lot of sense, but the woman was scary, so he did what she asked. That had been at six-twenty. That solved the case of how she got in there if Sunny locked it. Michele must have tried the doors to get her phone between six and before Evelyn showed back up around six-fifteen.

Lastly, I read Jo Jo Corman's statement. He went home after rehearsals. He said he had dinner with his dad and didn't leave his house the rest of the evening. Brady corroborated Jo Jo's account. I worried my lower lip between my teeth. Brady had been awfully worried for Jo Jo after I told him about Evelyn's murder. Hmmm. Alibi. Big question mark.

"Damn it." I set the files down.

"Find something?" Tyler asked.

"No," I lied. I had to find out why Brady was afraid for Jo Jo. Afraid enough to lie for him. I didn't see the kid as a murderer, but that didn't mean he wasn't. I can't tell you how many people over the years I've interviewed that said things like, I would have never suspected, he was always a nice guy, etc., etc. If Jo Jo was guilty, I'd have to turn him in. Maybe he had a good reason for killing Evelyn Meyers, but there was no way a therian court would look past the staged body.

Shit, shit, and more shit.

CHAPTER THIRTEEN

I **texted Brady and asked** him if he wanted to meet me for lunch. He said he was starting a bathroom addition for a client, but he could get away for an hour around one-thirty, did I want to meet at his house?

My fingers shook as I texted **yes**. I knew I'd be cutting it close to my scheduled meeting with Milo Greene, but I had a feeling Brady would be asking me to leave before the hour was up.

I grew queasy on the drive out to his house. How in the world could I ask him about Jo Jo without sounding like I was accusing him of aiding and abetting a criminal? I didn't want to believe the kid could kill and then pin Evelyn to a wall. I didn't get that vibe, but I had seen how angry he'd gotten at the rehearsals. What if Jo Jo had a temper that he'd been able to hide from everyone—everyone except his dad.

Blowing up my love life before it even had time to

sprout legs was not how I'd imagined my week going. At all.

I pulled into Brady's gravel drive, rocks crunching under my tires. Apprehension filled me until I thought I'd explode anxiety all over the dashboard.

Pull yourself together, Wilhelmina Boden. This was not me. This was not how I behaved. I'd become the head security officer for the Tri-State Council because I knew how to separate my personal life from work.

Yeah, said my inner voice. *But, as Ruth pointed out, you never cared about your personal life before now.*

I wanted to yank out my stupid inner voice and strangle it. Mostly because it was right.

Brady opened his front door and smiled at me. He wore a white t-shirt that hugged his broad chest, and a pair of jeans that made me purr. My stomach dropped. I didn't really need to know what he was hiding about Jo Jo, did I?

I had to remind myself that a woman was dead. The killer was the bad guy, not me. I had to follow the lead even if it meant losing my shot with Brady.

However, nothing said I couldn't ease into the implication that Jo Jo was suspect number one at this point. I turned off the engine and got out of the truck.

"Hi," I said. "What's cookin', good lookin'?" I inwardly groaned as more IQ points slipped away.

Brady chuckled. He tilted his head, gazing at me in a way that reminded me of my neighbor's pooch when the dog found something curious. It was adorable. "I'm frying up some hamburgers. How do you take yours?"

"Medium rare."

"Good, that's the way I like mine, too. I can take them out of the pan at the same time."

"Nice." An unnatural giddiness welled up inside me as I followed into the house. Finally, I'd get to see his home. The smell of juicy beef, sautéed onions, and garlic perfumed the living room. "It smells fantastic." The couch and chair were light blue chenille, and as I got closer, I detected the scent of detergent. The furniture had been recently cleaned. I reached down and touched the carpet. Damp. It had been shampooed. An old entertainment stand, full of scratches and scuff marks had been wiped down with lemon oil. Pictures of Jo Jo from infancy until he was about seven years old filled one wall. My heart sunk when I saw the family portrait: Brady, Rose Ann, and baby Jo Jo. They'd been a happy family before tragedy struck. It was the only picture of Rose Ann out in the open. I wondered if he kept the rest in his bedroom like a shrine.

Brady stepped out of the kitchen. "Burgers are ready. I hope you brought an appetite."

"I never leave home without it." I pushed aside my morbid thoughts and focused on the task at hand. Satisfy hunger first, curiosity second, and third, ruin my shot with Brady.

He placed the burgers on sweet buns that he'd buttered and grilled. We sat at a square dinner table with a slit in the middle for a leaf. There was a high back chair on each side, and two against the far wall. Mustard, catsup, mayo, pickles, sliced tomatoes, and sliced onions were already on the table.

Brady's kitchen was far bigger than I expected. "You

could put my whole living room and kitchen in your kitchen," I said.

"Rose Ann insisted on a large kitchen. Some people don't like company when they cook, but she loved having company around." He blinked at me. "Does it bother you if I talk about her?"

"No. Not at all." Maybe. She was his past, but it wasn't like he'd divorced her. If she'd lived, they would probably still be together. In that context, it was hard not to feel a little jealous. "I'd like to know more about you, about your life. She had a big part in shaping who you are today. I can't be mad about that. I think you're pretty great."

"I think you're pretty great, too."

"Now that we've started our mutual admiration club let's get down to the serious business of digging into these yummy burgers." I fixed my burger with mayo and catsup, pickles, and tomato. My taste buds exploded with the first bite. Every bit of the burger was seasoned to perfection, and the sweet-salty roll had me salivating for more. I debated for a minute whether it was better than an orgasm.

Nah. But it was a close second.

"Damn it, man, this is a fucking awesome hamburger." My mouth was still full, and a piece of bun fell onto my plate. Embarrassed, I picked it up and crammed it into my mouth.

He watched me from the other side of the table, a pleased smile tugging at his lips. "You eat the way you interrogate suspects. Aggressively. It's sexy."

I choked on a laugh, and another piece of burger

escaped my mouth. "Don't make me laugh," I said. "Not while I'm eating. I take my food very seriously."

"I can tell." He stood, picked up his napkin, leaned across the table, and wiped the corner of my mouth.

"Am I drooling?" Because, whoa baby, with Brady this near, drooling was a distinct possibility.

"No drool. Just some mayo." He sat back down.

"I'm not fit to be around civilized people."

"It's a good thing I'm not civilized."

I snorted. "Right. You were the mayor of this town, and before that, you practiced law. It doesn't get much more civilized than that."

His expression grew serious. "And I lived in the bottom of a liquor bottle for almost ten years after that. Being a lawyer. A leader. Those days are over for me." Brady rubbed his chin. "I don't know why I said all that. It's called Alcoholics Anonymous for a reason."

"How long have you been sober?"

"If I make it, I'll get my two-year chip in August."

I set my burger down on my plate. "Why wouldn't you make it?"

"Some days are worse than others, but stopping didn't make the urge go away."

"My dad was straight-laced my whole life. I never even saw him drink a beer, let alone any kind of hard liquor. I'd experimented with drinking briefly, but I didn't enjoy feeling out of control." I poked a finger in the top of my bun, unable to meet Brady's gaze. "I guess I'm telling you this, so you understand just how little I know about what it means to be an alcoholic. I know it's an addiction, but I won't pretend to know how you feel or what it takes to keep you sober." I glanced up from my plate, his amber eyes piercing me with their intensity. "Am I a problem? Does being around me make you want to drink?"

"Yes," he said. "And no."

"You're going to have to explain that one to me."

Brady got up and walked around to my side of the table. He knelt next to my chair and placed his hand on my knee. "When I met you last June, my worst fears were being realized. I'd already lost Rose Ann, and I'd almost managed to lose my son. I wanted nothing more that morning than to crawl into a vat of whiskey and drown myself. After it was over, I wanted to drink." He shook his head. "I attended an AA meeting every night for two weeks before I could get my head straight enough to function. But once I got there, all I could think about was the ballsy redhead who'd offered me a cup of coffee on a really dark day."

I pressed my palm to Brady's cheek. He closed his eyes briefly and leaned into my touch. When he opened his eyes, he smiled. "I couldn't get you out of my head. It drove me crazy."

"I have that effect on people."

Brady turned his face and kissed my palm. "Well, thinking about you like that made me want to drink even more. Though to be fair, some days all it takes is a bad weather forecast to get me there." He took my hand with his and interlaced our fingers. "You see, I'd been mourning my wife for two years. The guilt I felt about doubting her, for believing rumors about her, and to find out..." He closed his eyes again as he remembered the pain. "I held on to the grief. I made a promise to a ghost, a promise I mean to keep, and my guilt kept me sober. But when I think of you, the grief ebbs, I forget the remorse for a second, but when I remember, man, when I remember, that's when it really hits me."

"I'm not trying to take her place in your life."

"I know, but in some ways, I felt like I was trying to replace her in my life with you. Which is not your fault. You hadn't done anything but bring me a cup of coffee."

I turned in my seat, and Brady positioned himself between my legs, his forearms resting on my thighs. The conversation, while decidedly not sexy, did not mar my libido's reaction to him at all.

He reached around my back, his hand sliding up my spine until he cupped the back of my head. I moved with him, our lips meeting in a press of mutual desire. "I don't want to mess you up. I don't want to make your life worse," I murmured.

He smiled and leaned back so I could see his face. "That's just it. You don't make things worse. Not anymore. I think that's what scared me back in October. When we kissed, it felt right. I forgot what it was like to be..."

As he groped for a word, I supplied the one Ruth had used. "Happy."

He smiled. "Yeah, happy."

"Does it feel weird making out in Rose Ann's kitchen?"

He laughed. "This hasn't been her kitchen for a long time, but yes, maybe a little."

"So, maybe we should just eat lunch for right now." I eased away from Brady.

He sat back on his haunches. "Did I ruin this?"

"You haven't ruined a thing." But he had given me a lot to think about. "I just don't want this delicious food going to waste." Our luncheon had turned into true confessions, and since I'd already killed the mood, I decided to ask the hard questions. "So, Billy Bob thinks Evelyn's murder took place between six-fifteen and seven o'clock." I blew out a breath. "Do you believe your son was involved?"

Brady's expression flattened and stood up abruptly. "I know my son. He didn't have anything to do with this."

Brady returned to his chair. He stared at his hamburger but didn't pick it up. Well, he'd lost his appetite. *Good job, Willy.* And all that talk of staying off booze haunted me now. Would my questions push him over the edge? I had to believe Brady was stronger than that.

"You thought differently two nights ago, right? Talk to me," I said softly. "Maybe I can help, whatever the truth is."

He glanced at me, his expression pained. "I want to, Willy. I really do."

"You can trust me."

"Can I? You're the Tri-State Council investigator. You can't withhold evidence from the investigation, can you?" He studied my face. "That's what I thought. You don't have to hide what you don't know."

As I watched his facial expressions run the gambit of emotions, I was suddenly struck with an epiphany. I would keep his secrets. If Brady wanted me to, I would lie. I would withhold. I would do anything necessary to keep him from feeling one more moment of pain. What was wrong with me? Why did Brady affect me this way? I didn't know. These kinds of emotions were new, not to mention this strange resolve to protect Brady and his son.

"Nothing stays hidden for long," I said. "It's better to get out in front of the problem before it becomes too big to reconcile. If Jo Jo didn't have anything to do with Evelyn's murder, let's prove it." I reached across the table and took his hand. "Tell me the truth, Brady. I'll keep Jo Jo safe. I swear it."

Brady gripped my hand. "He came home around nine o'clock. He had blood on his shirt and pants. His right hand was swollen and bruised. He'd been in some kind of tussle."

"So, he lied to the police." Jo Jo said he'd gone right home after rehearsal and didn't leave the house.

"He asked me to cover for him, so I did." His jaw tightened. "He's my son."

"I understand." I squeezed his hand. "Did you clean the furniture and floors to hide evidence?"

Brady's eyes widened, and a sly, embarrassed smile crossed his lips. "Christ, no. That was for your benefit. I cleaned last night hoping you might stop by. This house has had two men living in it exclusively for over a decade. I couldn't get all the stains out of the sofa, but cushions turn."

I snorted a laugh. "I'll buy that." I paused. "Did you ask Jo Jo what happened?"

"I did. He told me he didn't want to talk about it. That

night, after you told me about Evelyn, I asked him if he had anything to do with it. He told me he didn't. I believe him. Whatever Jo Jo got himself into earlier in the evening, killing that woman wasn't part of it."

I nodded. "I believe you. And him."

"Yeah?"

"Yes. Evelyn had no defensive marks. No sign of a real struggle. The blood from the sword was minimal since the puncture happened when her circulatory system had been completely compromised, and she was close to death. Other than that, she had no open wounds. Where ever Jo Jo got that blood and those bruises, it wasn't in the process of killing the town jerk."

The burden of worry eased from his eyes. "I can live with that." He got up again and rounded the table to me. He picked me up with an ease that made me giggle and kissed me soundly. We made out like two love-sick yet virginal teens with a lot of over-the-clothes petting. I had to admit, the anticipation excited the shit out of me.

When we finally came up for air, Brady asked, "Can I take you out again tonight?"

"Absolutely." I looked at the clock on the microwave. It said it was two-forty-eight. "Is that right?"

"Yes."

My appointment with Milo Greene was at three o'clock. "Shoot! I have to get to the bank."

CHAPTER FOURTEEN

*D*riving **while horny** should be illegal. I found myself constantly distracted by shivers and tingles from memories of Brady's mouth on mine, his hands on my body, and his sexy groans as he smooshed his jean-clad parts against me. So much so, I missed the turn to the bank and had to go up another block to turn around.

I rushed inside, already a few minutes late. There was a receptionist behind a circular desk on the right-hand side as I entered. To the left, there was a long counter with four openings but only three tellers. I noted the three offices. Two were for loan officers, and the third had Milo Greene's name on it.

The receptionist, a woman named Sally with nutmeg hair in an A-line cut, stretched her lips into a tired smile. "Can I help you?"

"I'm here to see Mr. Greene. I had a three o'clock appointment."

Her eyebrows rose.

"I know I'm a little late. Would you let him know I'm here?"

"Sure. Have a seat."

I read a People Magazine from 2015 for ten minutes. What was it with celebrity relationships? They traded in spouses like most people did cars. Finally, the receptionist waved me over. "I'm sorry. Mr. Greene isn't available. Would you like to reschedule your meeting?"

"Of course." I pulled out my Tri-State Council Security badge and showed it to her. "Mr. Greene can meet me at the sheriff's department for an official interview about Evelyn's death. How about tonight after he gets off work?"

"He...uh, well, let me see if he can squeeze you in." Sally toddled on high heels as she hurried to Milo's office. Two minutes later, she stepped out. In a conspiratorial tone, she said, "Mr. Greene says he'll push back his other appointments and see you now."

"That's mighty kind of him." I tipped my chin to Sally and walked into Greene's office.

Milo Greene stood as I entered. He wore a tan suit that fit his slender build and narrow shoulders. It wasn't off the rack, but it wasn't high end either. It screamed upper-middle-class businessman. He had chestnut brown hair, cut short and neat. His bushy brows curtained his hazel-blue eyes. "Ms. Boden, do come in."

"I'm in," I told him, closing the door behind me.

My response threw him off balance, but he quickly recovered. "I'm sorry for the mix-up. I'm happy to talk to any investigator for the Council."

Sunny had been right about the badge opening doors.

"I'm happy to hear that. I'm sure President Stenson will be pleased to hear about your eagerness to cooperate." Not that I had any intention of telling the Council leader about Milo unless what he told me impacted the case. "When did you last see the victim, Evelyn Meyers?" I knew what he'd told Deputy Connelly, but I wanted to hear the account from his mouth.

His gaze flickered up for a second. "We finished rehearsals at six o'clock. I didn't talk to Evel—Ms. Meyers," he amended, "except to the discuss the play. I drove home right after, and I didn't leave my house the rest of the evening."

"Where is your house in relation to Ms. Meyers' home?"

He grunted at the question. "Well, my wife and I live in the house right next to hers. On the right," he added.

I recalled that one being the double deck with a gazebo. I frowned. "And you went straight home."

"Yes."

"You didn't see anyone next door at her house?"

"No, after a long day, I can sometimes get engrossed in the television."

"Is that what you did that night?"

"What?"

"Get engrossed in television?"

"Uhm, yes."

"What did you watch?"

His posture stiffened. "These questions seem unnecessary."

"I'll decide what's unnecessary, Mr. Greene. Now, what did you watch?"

He clenched his jaw and broke eye contact. "South Park," he mumbled.

"What?"

"I was watching old episodes of South Park on SetFlicks." He gave me a look that dared me to laugh, so I did. His discomfort was due to good old-fashioned embarrassment. "I find Kenny and his friends relaxing," he said, his voice defensive.

"I'm not judging." I had my own SetFlicks subscription, and I've watched shows I'd never admit to in adult company. "You and Ms. Meyers were neighbors. Were you friends?"

"Evel—Ms. Meyers didn't have friends." He pinched the bridge of his nose. "I'll be honest, Ms. Boden. I didn't know Evelyn that well."

First, I was a firm believer that when a person prefaced a statement with "I'll be honest," it usually meant they were being anything but honest, and the fact that Milo Greene struggled to not use Evelyn's first name told me he didn't want me to know just how well he knew her. "Did Ms. Meyers keep her money here at Peculiar Community?"

"Yes, I believe she did. Most of the locals bank with us."

I studied his office. There was a portrait of Milo with a blonde woman with a heart-shaped face and turned up nose. "Is that your wife?"

"Yes." He gave me a tight-lipped smile.

"Is she friends with Ms. Meyers?"

His abrupt, "No," pulled me up short. His reaction went far beyond embarrassment about his TV viewing choices. He was hiding something.

"And if I wanted to talk to Mrs. Greene, would she be at home this afternoon?"

Milo shifted uncomfortably in his seat. "My wife is staying with her parents right now. She went back this morning."

Trouble in paradise? "Why is that?"

"Her mother hasn't been well," he said. He straightened, trying to appear indignant. "I find this whole line of questioning distasteful and irrelevant."

"As I said earlier, I'll decide what's important." I noticed a brightly colored bird figurine on his desk. It looked similar to the one I saw in Evelyn's home office. "What kind of bird is this?"

Milo sucked his teeth in annoyance. "I have no idea." He slid open his desk drawer and put the figurine inside. If it wasn't important, why would he feel the need to hide a desk trinket? "I have work to do, Ms. Boden. Are we through?"

"No. Did you handle Ms. Meyers money personally?"

"I told you I barely knew the woman."

"You barely knew a woman who had close to a million dollars in your bank?"

"What makes you think Ms. Meyers has that much money?"

I couldn't exactly tell him about the accounting books, so I let my silence do the talking.

"If she does," he finally said. "I don't know anything about it."

"You'll excuse me if I find that hard to believe. I've been in Peculiar enough to know that there aren't many folks in town with that kind of scratch."

"Are you calling me a liar?"

"Are you a liar, Mr. Greene?"

He ignored the question. "I can't give you information about our customers or their accounts."

"Until I get a warrant."

Milo stood up, obviously rattled. He fished a card from his desk. "If you have any more questions for me, call my solicitor."

"Why do you need a lawyer?" I asked as I got up and took the card. "Did you kill Evelyn?"

He paled. "No, I did not. I know my rights. I don't have to talk to you."

"You know your human rights, sure. But you must also follow therian laws, and they're quite different."

"Either way, I'm entitled to a lawyer. If you need anything else, contact Harrison Walker. He's in Osage Beach."

"This Walker guy, is he an integrator?"

"Yes, he's an opossum therian, so he knows all about shifter laws."

I curled my lip. "Fine. I expect you'll bring him to your follow-up interview." At the door, I turned back, and added, "Oh, and I'll be sure to let President Stenson know just how cooperative you were."

Milo blanched, but he didn't ask me to stay. I moved him to the top of my suspect list. First, he didn't have an alibi, and second, he lied about how well he knew Evelyn, and third, he lied about knowing how much money she had.

I exited the bank and jumped into my truck. Evelyn Meyers' house deserved a second look, and now that I was officially on the case, I could pick up the bank book and give it the thorough exam it deserved. I grabbed my phone and called the Sheriff's Department. Eldin Farraday answered. The evening shift must have started already.

"I'm going out to Meyer's place. Do you all have the key?"

"We already gave it a once over."

"I know. I can't shake the feeling we missed something."

"You mean, you think we missed something." Eldin grew quiet for a moment, and then said, "I'll meet you out there."

When I arrived at Stony Park Villa, I parked next to the curb in front of Evelyn's house. A forest green compact car was parked in the driveway. Would Eldin drive his personal car?

I got out of the truck. Nicole, the sheriff's daughter, stood by the front door to the house.

"Hello," I called. She turned, startled.

She pulled out her earbuds. "Hey," she said. "Sorry, audiobook." She indicated the buds. "I get caught up sometimes."

"No problem. What are you doing out here?"

"Dad said it was okay." She had a set of keys in her

hand. "I told mom I'd pick out an outfit for Evelyn for the funeral."

"Doctor Smith hasn't released the body yet, has he?"

"He will eventually. I am trying to take care of as much stuff as I can so my mom doesn't have to do it herself."

I followed Nicole to the front entrance. She unlocked the door. "I'm sure Jean is grateful to have you home." Sid had said she'd just graduated with her Ph.D. "What are your plans now that you're out of college?" I had a four-year criminal justice degree and five months of police academy training, so I was familiar with the dedication it took for Nicole to finish an advanced degree.

"My plans are up in the air right now."

I thought it strange that someone smart enough to get into a Stanford Ph.D. program didn't have her entire future mapped out.

She held the door open for me, and we went inside. "Do you mind if I look through her closet and bureau before you?"

Nicole shrugged. "Sure, I'm not in any hurry."

The master bedroom was on the main floor at the back of the hallway past the office, a utility closet, and a guest bathroom. I started with the walk-in closet. Evelyn had kept it neat and tidy like the rest of the house. She organized by style rather than color. Evening dresses, professional clothes, casual shirts, slacks, jeans, etc. It wasn't overly fussy like someone with OCD, but it lacked the chaos of my closet. She had a shoe rack mounted on the back wall, with various heels, loafers, three pairs of tennis shoes, some booties, and a half-dozen sandals. There were a variety of colors and styles. The shoes were worn, nothing brand new. I've never been a clothes hound, but if I had Evelyn's money, who knows. But she didn't spend like someone who had a million bucks.

I found a step-stool folded next to the shoe rack. I opened it and stepped up to look at the shelves over the clothes rods. Evelyn had vacuum-packed comforters, quilts, and extra pillows in neat stacks. The only non-bedding item was a small, rose decoupage box with a dark pink lid. I retrieved it and got off the stool.

"What did you find?" Nicole asked.

"It's a box." I put it on the bed and lifted the lid. A stack of pictures, notes, letters, and other little treasures filled the container.

Nicole let out a noisy exhalation. I looked at her. "Sorry," she said, a nervous giggle bubbling to the surface. "I guess I was holding my breath. I didn't know what we'd find in there."

"Were you worried she kept a severed head in it?"

Nicole laughed. "Maybe. This is my Aunt Evelyn we're talking about. I wouldn't be surprised if we found literal skeletons in the closet."

"You weren't close?"

"No. She made it perfectly clear that my mom and dad were scum. She tolerated me better than some, but the woman had a very rigid view of most people." Nicole reached into the box and pulled out the stack of photos before I could stop her. "Hey, that's my dad. Man, he looks so young here."

"Is that your mom next to him?" I pointed at the woman next to a really handsome Sid.

"It looks kind of like her, but, no, I think it's Evelyn."

Uh oh. "Were your mom and her sister close growing up?"

"I have no idea. My folks didn't talk much about Aunt Ev, and the little they did say was never flattering." Nicole gave me an apprehensive look. "I know this sounds bad, but I promise you, my mom cared for Evelyn. Her sister's death has affected her, so don't think she or my dad are glad that Evelyn's dead."

"Jean is in some of these pictures," I tugged one out and showed Nicole the photo. The sisters stood in front of a house I could only assume belonged to their parents. Jean and Evelyn look like friends. I wonder what changed."

Nicole pushed her raven hair back behind her shoulders. I noticed little strands of white that would eventually become more abundant as she got older, giving her the salt and pepper appearance of her parents.

She put the pictures back in the box and closed the lid. "Whatever it was, happened before I was born. The past is the past for a reason."

But I knew from experience that someone's past often provided the motive for murder. Not even therians were immune from holding grudges.

"I'm done in the closet." I searched the dresser drawers next. She had dedicated drawers for socks, underwear, nightgowns, bras, and body shapers. I looked on her bedside stand when the bureau produced nothing notable. The nightstand proved to be more interesting. Evelyn had a vibrator, lubricant, feminine wipes, and a few pictures of herself wearing a black negligee in boudoir poses.

Nicole peered over my shoulder. "That's something you can't unsee." She grimaced. "Masturbation instruments ranks right up there with things you should never know about family members."

"I don't think it was all self-love for Evelyn," I told her.

"What do you mean?" Nicole moved around me to get a better look.

I picked up the box of feminine wipes. Under was a box of Magnum condoms, and it was open and half empty. "I don't think she was using these on her dildo."

Evelyn Meyers had a lover. But who? And why hadn't he come forward?

CHAPTER FIFTEEN

I left **Nicole in the** bedroom and headed to the office. "Willy?" Deputy Farraday said from the living room

"Here!" I answered.

He joined me in the hallway.

"How'd you get in?"

"Me," Nicole said, peeking her head out from the bedroom. "Dad gave me the key."

Eldin jangled the keys in his hand. "Hmm."

"I was just heading to the office to poke around. Want to join me?" I asked Farraday.

"Sure." He put the keys in his pocket and followed me down the hall.

We went into the first door on the right, and once I knew Nicole was out of earshot I said, "What was the hmm about?"

He shrugged. "Nothing."

"Don't give me that shit, Eldin. What is it about Nicole having keys that you didn't like?" I prodded.

"We only found one set of house keys. They were in Ms. Meyers purse."

"You all found the purse at the community center, right?"

"It was next to the queen's throne."

He was talking about the prop throne. "It's possible Evelyn gave her sister a set of keys in case she lost hers."

Eldin shrugged. "It's possible."

But the tension and distance between the two sisters made it improbable. I couldn't help but think about the pictures of Sid and Evelyn when they were younger and the half empty box of condoms.

I shook my head.

"What?" Eldin asked.

"Nothing."

He raised his brows, his expression amused. "Now who's dishing shit?"

"It's not that," I told him. "The idea in my head is so ludicrous it doesn't bear saying out loud."

"Say it anyway." His eyes, the silver-green color of juniper, held my gaze.

"Do you think Sheriff Taylor was having an affair with Evelyn?"

Eldin's eyes widened, his lips parting with surprise. He burst out laughing. He laughed so hard a tear rolled down his cheek.

"All right," I said sourly.

"What's going on?" Nicole asked. "Did you find something funny?"

"I found something funny, all right," Eldin wheezed. I smacked him on the arm and gave him a warning glare. I didn't want him repeating to Nicole what I'd asked about her dad. To cover, Eldin picked up the figurine of the colorful bird. "Why would Ms. Meyers only keep one love bird? They usually come as a set."

"What did you say?"

He turned the bird in his hand. "Lovebirds. I've seen these at a shop in Osage Beach. One of those tourist stores. The guy there sells them in sets."

I took the figurine from him. "I think I know where its mate is." I was also pretty sure I knew who'd been using those condoms. Milo Greene had a lot of explaining to do.

I walked to the other side of the desk and opened the middle drawer. "Sometimes these drawers have false bottoms." I hated how phony I sound, but I continued the act by tugging on the organizer part. I lifted up and feigned surprise when it moved. A moment later, the surprise was real. The space was empty. "Did you all take anything into evidence from the office?"

"I don't think so."

"No logs or files or anything like that?"

"No. We didn't find anything that pointed at a motive, so we left everything in place."

Not everything. The bank ledger was gone.

My thoughts drifted back to that picture of Sid and Evelyn. I didn't like what my gut was telling me. Was Sid tanking this investigation? I didn't want to consider the sheriff would commit murder, much less obstruct an investigation. But I couldn't dismiss him as a suspect, either.

Son-of-a-bitch.

IT WAS six by the time Eldin, and I finished combing the rest of the house. The upstairs was eerily unused. There were two bedrooms, a bathroom, and a studio. They were all furnished, but the closets and drawers were empty as if they were in a holding pattern until someone could fill them. Maybe that's how Evelyn felt, why else would she have an affair with a married man? Yes, I was speculating, but my instincts told me I was right about Greene and her.

On the way back to the Sheriff's Department, I saw Josh, Sabrina's son, standing on the curb carrying a backpack and furiously texting on his phone. I slowed down just as Roger Park roared up the street in his fancy car. Josh got in on the passenger side. The tint on Roger's window was still present. He hadn't taken it off like Farraday had told him to. I called the deputy, hoping he wasn't too far behind me.

"You up for a traffic stop?"

"What do you have in mind?"

"I just passed Roger Parks, and he still has illegal tinting on his windows."

"Which way is he heading?" Eldin sounded eager.

"He was on Holden heading north about half a minute ago." I turned my truck around. "I'll head north, you come in from the top. We'll stay on the phone until one of us sees him."

"Sounds like a plan." A few seconds later, Eldin said. "Got him. He turned off on Fifth Street heading east."

"Take him. I'll back you when I get there."

I heard the wail of sirens both over the phone and in the distance. I was close. I kept the phone on, not because I was worried for the deputy, but you just never knew how people might react when they felt cornered.

When I approached the scene, Roger had his window down, while Eldin wrote in his ticket pad. I got out of my truck and came up on the passenger side. I knocked on the window.

Farraday instructed him to roll his window down immediately. Josh complied, but he still wouldn't look at me.

"What are you up to today?"

"Nothing," he grunted and then shrugged.

"We're just cruising around. That's not against the law," Roger said.

"It is when you're doing it in a vehicle with aftermarket tint on the front windows and windshield," Farraday said. "I told you yesterday to take it off. You were warned."

"Where's your backpack, Josh?" I asked.

The kid's face turned ashen. "I...what backpack?"

"The one you had when you got in Roger's car back on Holden Street." I poked my head into the window, getting in the kid's space and checked the backseat. No backpack. Where would they have ditched it? It wasn't like they'd been out of sight for very long. "If I search down the street am I going to find a black and brown backpack, Josh?"

"How do I know what you're going to find?"

"You talk to your momma that way?"

Josh flinched and then squirmed under my cop stare. "I don't have a backpack," he maintained.

I wasn't getting anywhere with the little twerp. It was the problem with teenagers. They thought they were invincible, which made them stupid and reckless.

Farraday finished writing Roger's ticket. He ripped it off the pad and handed it to the sulky kid. The deputy looked at me across the roof of the car. "Are we done here?"

"For now." I gave both Roger and Josh my best I'm-watching-you glare.

As Roger pulled away, Eldin turned to me. "You're going to search Twelfth Street and Holden, aren't you?"

I smiled. "Yep. You busy?"

"Yep." He smiled back. "Busy finding a backpack."

It was ninety degrees in the shade outside. After forty minutes of searching yards and ditches, we were sweaty and no closer to finding a backpack than we'd been when we started.

"What a pisser," I said, wiping the perspiration off my face with the bottom of my shirt.

"You're a strange woman, Willy," Eldin said. "I dig it."

"I'm pretty sure you prefer Bambi over bobcats, but if you're game..." I wiggled my brows and laughed when his face turned red. "Don't worry, Foxy. I'm not hot after your tail. I've got a different predator in mind."

Eldin smirked. "Like I said, strange woman. I'm heading back to the station, you?"

"I'm calling it a day and going to shower. I no longer smell of sunshine and roses." I wrinkled my nose. "Call me if you get anything new on the case?"

"Sure thing."

My phone rang. I grabbed it from my purse. It was Brady. I promised myself I'd be cool and poised if he called. I swiped it to answer and put the phone to my ear.

"What's shakin' bacon?" Gah! Brady must think I had brain damage. "I mean, what's up?" Not much better.

"Hey, Willy." I could hear the smile in his voice. "Did I catch you at a bad time?"

"Nope. I was just fixing to go back to Ruth's."

"Can I pick you up in an hour? I want to take you for a picnic."

In this heat? I'd have to ask the Thompson ladies if any of them had industrial-strength antiperspirant. "I'd love that, but can you give me two hours? I'm going to have to scrub the day off me before I'm fit for anyone."

"You need some help with the loofah, you let me know."

"Why Brady Corman, you are making me blush." Not really, but I knew he'd be blushing now. I could hear it in his laugh.

Out of the corner of my eye, I caught a movement. I jerked my gaze to the left in time to see Josh Miller running across a nearby backyard with that damn black and brown backpack. Damn it. Chasing that kid would put a serious dent in my two-hour timeline.

"I have to go. Looking forward to tonight. Bye!" I hung up, shoved my phone in my purse, and took off after the lying juvenile delinquent.

Josh made me chase him for two blocks, me yelling for him to stop the whole time, before he threw his backpack over a privacy fence and ran the other way. I had to decide, did I keep after Josh and beat his ass for making me even stinkier before my date tonight? Or did I go for the backpack? I could potentially do both, but if I went after the kid, someone else might grab the pack.

Screw it. I'd contact Sabrina tomorrow, and she could bring him down to the station for a talk. The backpack took priority.

I'm a cat shifter, which meant, I'm a good jumper...in bobcat form. However, even in hominid form, I was still light on my feet. I grabbed the top of the six-foot wooden privacy fence and hoisted myself up and over. I landed in a crouch on the other side. A big fucking dog lunged at me, his vicious barking and growling giving me a minor heart attack, as I leaped sideways and out of his reach. I seriously wished I had thought to bring my go-pack with the doggie treats. Thank heavens, the gorgeous brute was on a chain. On the other hand, it was freaking hot outside today. What asshole left their dog outside on a chain all day in this hellish weather?

"Dagger," a guy yelled as the glass door on the back of the house slid open. "Shut up!"

Roger Freakin' Park. His douchebaggery knew no bounds. What kind of therian allowed his dog to suffer in the heat? A therian knew what it was like to exist in animal form. The little shit saw me a moment later. "Hey! What are you doing in my yard?"

I picked up the bag. "Get your dog inside, asshole. It's hot as balls out here." And on that note, I grabbed the top of the fence again and launched myself over to the other side. I could still hear Roger yelling multiple expletives as I jogged back to the truck.

Hah! At least, now that I had the bag, I could find out what Josh and Roger tried to hide. When I got it back to my vehicle, I set the backpack on the seat and unzipped it. My confusion compounded as I stared at what appeared to be several coils of quarter-inch herringbone metal chain.

CHAPTER SIXTEEN

*W*hy the hell had Josh tried to ditch a bag full of metal chain? Had he stolen it from somewhere? Was there even a market for this kind of thing? Maybe it was a new teen kink I hadn't heard of yet.

These were the questions going through my mind while I scrubbed down in Ruth's master bathroom shower. Along with, *should I shave my legs? If I shave my legs am I being presumptuous about the date? Should I shave my bikini area? I should definitely shave the bikini area*. It didn't matter whether Brady went to the third base or not, there was no sense in taking a chance he might get lost in the current jungle down there. The pits were a no-brainer. That stubble was the first to go.

I was going on a picnic. My turbocharged heartbeat started making my chest hurt. At one point while I was washing my hair, I got light-headed. Why was I getting all worked up? So, I liked Brady. Maybe more than liked

Brady, but guess what? He liked me, too, or he wouldn't have asked me out for a picnic. Right?

God, when did I turn into a thirteen-year-old girl?

After my shower, I dressed in a pair of jean shorts and a pale green camisole. I'd tied my hair with the towel to absorb the excess water. Getting my hair date ready was a whole long and involved process. There were times when thick hair really created a time-suck.

"Green really brings out your eyes," Ruth said.

"Does yellow?"

Ruth raised her brow in question.

"You know, yellow belly. I'm scared as shit."

"About what?"

"About the fact that I'd never dated a man I didn't ditch because I don't know how to have a relationship." I took the towel off my head and grabbed the blow dryer from the vanity. "I've run from them all my life." I waved the blow dryer like a mad woman. "The minute the guy gets serious, I get the hell out. What if that happens again? What if the minute Brady stops acting coy, I decide I don't want him anymore?

Ruth giggled.

I aimed the blow dryer at her. "It's not funny. This is serious, Ruth."

"I can tell," she said. "You're really worked up."

"Yes, I am!" I stared at her, my hands shaking, the dryer still pointed at her.

Ruth burst out laughing. She raised both her hands. "Don't shoot."

I lowered the dryer, "Stop it," I whined.

"I'm sorry, sorry," she wheezed, still laughing.

"I'm pathetic."

Ruth held her thumb and forefinger an inch apart. "Little bit." She threw her arms around me. "Have I told you how happy I am that you're here? It's been a long time since I've had this much fun."

She was a little taller than me, but I rose on my tiptoes, put my chin on her shoulder, and hugged her back. "I'm not sure this qualifies as fun. You may need to re-evaluate your idea of a good time."

Ruth gave me a pat and leaned back. "I think you need to re-evaluate your relationship fears." She picked up a thick wet curl from my shoulder. "You better get on this, or you'll be going on your date with damp hair."

"Wait," I said before she could leave me. "Do you think I'm bad for Brady?"

"Oh, honey." Ruth sighed the sigh I'd heard her use with her children when telling them something obvious. "You're not afraid you're going to break Brady's heart."

"I'm not?"

"No." She shook her head. "You're afraid he's going to break yours."

I took a second to process and nodded. "You're one smart cookie, Ruth Thompson."

She grinned. "You would have eventually got there."

"Hey, Mom." Michele popped her head in the door. "Hey, Willy."

I guess she wasn't mad at me anymore. Score one for me.

"There's a man at the door. He wants to speak to Willy."

"Is it Brady?"

"No. He says his name is Richard Stenson." She shrugged.

"Oh, dear," Ruth said.

"What the hell is he doing here?"

Michele came in the room, closed the door behind her, her expression fierce. "If he's some stalker ex-boyfriend, tell me, and I will kick him to the curb."

"None of that," Ruth said. She ushered Michele to the door. "Go put President Stenson into the kitchen. Offer him some pie and coffee, and tell him Willy will be out shortly."

"What the fuck is he doing here?" I asked.

"He didn't say anything to you?"

"The last time we talked, Stenson told me to investigate Evelyn's murder. That's it. He didn't say anything about driving down here himself."

"I guess there's only one way to find out."

"Well, double shit." I wasn't going to have time to do my hair. I twisted the wet mess into a high bun and frowned at Ruth. "You got some pins?"

RICHARD STENSON SAT at the kitchen table gobbling down a piece of blackberry pie. He looked up at me when I walked into the kitchen, a dark-purple berry piece hanging from his thick, white-blond mustache. He finished chewing and swallowed his mouthful and gestured with his spoon for me to sit down.

"This is some great pie," he said.

I rubbed my upper lip to mirror where the berry filling clung to him. Stenson didn't catch on.

"President Stenson, this is unexpected."

"I'd like a progress report on the Evelyn Meyers case." He took another scoop of pie with a bit of vanilla ice cream.

"I was planning to call you in the morning. I have a few leads, but nothing concrete." I held up my hands. "I wish I had more to tell you."

He shook his head, the filling glob precariously close to dropping on his shirt. "I'm supposed to have a meeting with the mayor, the sheriff, and Doctor Smith tomorrow. I'd like you to join me."

"Yes, sir. Can I ask why?"

"Isn't it enough that a prominent member of this community has been killed?"

"Sure, but therians get killed all the time. This is the first one that you've taken an interest in."

He narrowed his light blue gaze on me. "This is the first one where I've had a personal interest in the case. Last month, Evelyn Meyers informed me about a scam that was taking place in Peculiar. I have since found out that it has far-reaching implications for other therianthrope communities. It is a poison. A cancer that needs to be excised."

Which was pretty far away from the original reason he'd sent me to Peculiar. Not that I'd done any real investigation on Sunny. Still, Stenson's sudden appearance in town and his switch of mission goals surprised me. "Why wasn't I given this new information?"

"I needed to verify Ms. Meyer's claims independently. I wanted you in Peculiar to keep an eye on things."

The machinations of the therian political community made me crazy. Instead of just saying, go hang out in town and let me know if you see anything strange, he'd sent me off on a wild goose chase about Sunny. I didn't think he knew that Sunny was a human, or this would be a whole different conversation.

"And how does Sunny Trimmel fit into all of this?"

His face grew pinched. "Evelyn didn't give me details. Only that it involved several Peculiar locals, including someone connected and very well-respected." He leaned forward, and the berry-dingle fell onto his plate. Absently, he licked the pie juice from the furry caterpillar above his lip. "Mrs. Trimmel is fairly new to the town. Have you noticed any suspicious behavior in her?"

"No. Between directing the community play, running her restaurant, and raising two kids, I don't think she has time to implement evil plans."

"What about Doctor Smith, the Sheriff, or the Mayor?

"Nope. I haven't noticed anything." Out of those three, only Sid's behavior bordered on suspicious.

Stenson flicked his gaze upward at me. "You've always been a solid investigator. My predecessor and fellow Council members have had the utmost faith in your capabilities. Your stint with the FBI has made you an asset."

"I know how to get a job done," I said dryly.

"That's what I like to hear." He leaned back and patted his stomach. Stenson stood up. His narrow framed reminded me of a pale blond Ichabod Crane from the Sleepy Hollow story. He went to the sink and washed his hands. Used a paper towel to dry his hands and wipe his mouth. "I'll expect you at the mayor's office tomorrow at eight-fifty in the morning. The appointment's at nine, but I'd like us to enter together." He rubbed his brow then gave his head a slight shake. "And please dress business appropriate."

When Stenson left, Michele bumped my shoulder. "That guy is wound tighter than my momma's cookie jar lid."

I snickered. "True story, my friend." I looked at the teenage girl on the verge of adulthood and gave her the nod. "We good?"

"Yes. I'm sorry I overreacted."

At that, I snorted. "More like over-acted."

"Yeah, yeah." She grinned sheepishly. "Boys'll make you crazy."

A knock at the door had me standing at attention. "Another true story," I said.

Linus sprinted past us, wearing white flip-flops, green and purple polka-dotted shorts, and no shirt. "I got it," he yelled as if someone was going to race him to the door.

"Who dresses that kid?"

"Good Will," Michele said. When I gave her a look, she added, "Seriously, when mom takes us shopping in

Lake Ozarks, Linus insists on going to the Good Will store."

"He can wear whatever he pleases," Ruth said. She wrapped her arms around her daughter from behind and kissed the girl's cheek. "I make it a point not to judge my children's appearances. Otherwise, Michele here wouldn't have spent three months of her fourth-grade year wearing rainbow-colored rain boots to school every day."

"I wish you would have," Michele said. "Some people still call me Shelly Welly."

"Better than Smelly Shelly," I noted.

Michele squinted at me.

I held up a hand. "Just saying."

"Mr. Corman's here!" Linus yelled as he ran past us the opposite way, his flip-flops slapping against his heels with every step.

Brady strolled inside. His eyes met mine, and those amber orbs gazed at me with fevered intent.

"It just got hot in here," Michele said.

Ruth took hold of her daughter's arm. "Uhm, let's leave Willy and Mr. Corman alone."

I barely noticed them go. Brady looked as yummy as ever. He'd shaved his five o'clock shadow, and without it, he looked young. Fresh. Like a man who hadn't almost destroyed his life. Like a man I wanted to kiss. Badly.

He wiped his palms on the front of his cobalt blue t-shirt. "Damn, woman, you make my palms sweat."

"And hello to you," I said, my voice shy. At least I hadn't said, "What's crack-a-lackin'?" or some other inane greeting. "You look nice."

"You look..." The tip of his tongue briefly licked his lower lip.

"Good enough to eat?"

He chuckled. "And then some." He gestured toward the door. "You ready?"

"Yes. Let me grab my purse, and we can go." Wee haw! I was going on a picnic. I ran upstairs. The backpack was next to a pile of my dirty clothes. I should probably drop it off at the police station, but I figured it would keep until morning.

I forced myself not to race downstairs singing Rod Stewart's *Tonight's the Night*. It was a picnic. At night. Under the stars. I swooned at the thought. Most of my dates considered dinner at Buffalo Wild Wings a romantic night out.

When I got back downstairs, Brady held out his hand. Giddy as a school girl, I took it. He held the door open for me and gave me a boost up into his truck. After, he closed the door and went around the front to the driver's side.

Before he started the truck, he said, "Oh, hey, before I got distracted by your...uhm, beautiful eyes, he gave me a courtesy once over, and I grinned. "That guy who I saw leaving Ruth's. Do you know who he is?"

"That was the illustrious Richard Stenson. He took over for Lowry as the Tri-State Council president. Why?"

"About two weeks ago, I showed up at Evelyn's about an hour early. I'd wanted to get an early start on the day because of the heat. I saw that fella leaving Evelyn's driveway as I pulled into Stony Park."

"You sure?"

"Positive. That mustache is hard to mistake."

"Well, shit." It seemed like while I was holding things back from Stenson, he was holding things back from me. "That's not good."

CHAPTER SEVENTEEN

"**So, where we going?**" I asked Brady after we'd been driving for about twenty minutes deeper and deeper into the backcountry.

"I have a cabin out here by a lake. I bought it as a place to shift and run." He shook his head. "And drink when I needed a different kind of running." He cast a sideways glance at me. "I've cleaned it up, too. Just so you don't think I'm trying to hide any bodies."

He was so cute with his teasing that I had to laugh. "Don't you know? Good friends don't rat you out, they help you hide the bodies."

"Is that what we are?" He reached over and slid his fingers between mine. "Good friends?"

My mouth went dry as I worked on getting my breathing under control. Christ, having this man touch me, even something so simple as holding my hand, was like taking a seltzer bath. Everything tingled. "Yes," I managed to say. "The best."

"Excellent." Brady squeezed my hand, and it made my little Willy, aka my va-jay-jay clench. And, damn it, I could smell the musk of my arousal. A low growl rumbled in Brady's chest. Apparently, he could smell me too.

I blushed. Lord have mercy, you'd think I was a virgin the way I was acting. But for whatever reason, Brady made me feel like one. He made me feel like whatever happened between us, it would be my first time.

When I tried to pull my hand from his, he squeezed tighter. The weight of his possession revved my engines. "How long is it going to take to get to this cabin?"

"About thirty seconds." He did a one-armed turn down a small gravel road. His feral grin set my nerves ablaze.

The sun hung low in the sky casting orange and gold hues over a large pond. A thicket of trees surrounded the banks, with an opening on our side where a small log cabin served as the only audience to its beauty. Some might say the place was isolated, but I called it Nirvana.

Brady brought my fingers to his lips and kissed the tips. "Do you like it?"

"Oh, yes," I said with too much breath. "It's stunning."

"I hoped you would." He got out of the truck, and before I could get my hands on the door handle, he was already there, offering his hand to help me out. I must have given him a queer look because he said, "I hope you don't mind. I haven't been on a date in over twenty years so you can tell me if I'm getting it wrong."

I went up on my tiptoes and placed a soft kiss on his lips. "You're getting everything just right."

He gazed down at me. The reflection of the setting sun

filled his irises with fire. "I'm glad you approve." He turned to the truck bed. "I'll get the food and blanket. Go find us a flat spot to set up."

"Oh, we really are having a picnic." I rubbed my hands together. "Yay. I'm starving."

"Woman, I have a feeling you'd be starving after a ten-course meal."

The way he said *woman* made me glad to be a woman. Oh, baby. Yes. "See, you know me so well already."

I found an area under a shade tree near the bank of the pond. Far enough back that the mosquitos would be less interested. Brady followed me down with a big woven basket and a thick blanket.

"Is here all right?" I asked.

"Perfect."

His approval thrilled me, which made my inner-feminist moan. *Shut up*, I told it. *I can get excited by this excellent specimen of a man if I want to, so there.*

He put down the basket and splayed out the blanket. "You have a seat."

I found a spot near the middle and got comfortable. I smiled when he popped the top on a bottle of cold root beer and handed it to me.

"How did you know I liked root beer?"

"You ordered it with your jackfruit burger the other day."

Oh, yeah. Aww. He'd paid attention. "Thanks."

"You enjoy the scene while I make us a fire." He walked back up to the truck and came down with a bundle of split wood and a smaller bundle of kindling.

He crouched several feet away—close enough for ambiance, but far enough away it wouldn't add to the sweltering heat—and built the kindling teepee. It gave me the ultimate view of his backside in those jeans. Rawr.

Brady, sweet, Brady, your perfectly muscled ass is all the fire I need. "You need any help over there?" I took a long sip of the root beer. "It sure looks like thirsty work." And, mamma, he was making me thirsty.

"I've got it." A serpentine flame crawled up the sticks.

"You sure do," I agreed.

He turned his hot gaze on me. "Are you ogling my ass?"

"As often as you let me." I grinned and took another swig of my drink. Then belched. Loudly. Longly. All kinds of wrongly. Suave, I wasn't. "Oops. Sorry."

"You are unexpected." With the kindling blazing, he started building another pyramid with the split logs.

"I could say the same about you." I leaned back on an elbow. "I was raised by a single father."

"Yeah?"

"Yep." I chanced another drink. "My mom left us shortly after Hans was born. She told my dad she needed to be free."

"That sucks."

"It really did. I had no one to teach me how to act like a girl, let alone a woman. My dad treated me like a son because he knew about boys. Girls were a mystery." I snorted a laugh. "That's probably why my mom left. And that's definitely why I got called Willy and not Wilhelmina, but really, what a mouthful that would have been to grow up with."

"Do you see her?"

"My mom?"

He nodded.

"No. But that don't bother me." I waved away a mosquito. "I'm not telling you this, so you'll feel sorry for me."

He'd finished the fire building and sat down on the blanket next to me. "Then why are you telling me?"

"Because I want you to know that I don't know how to be delicate, feminine. I don't cook, I certainly don't clean, I leave my laundry on the floor, I sometimes forget to shower unless I smell bad enough that I can't stand myself. I'm good at my job, but I'm not good at much else."

"Basically, you're a teenage boy."

"Without the penis and testosterone."

He chuckled. "That's something to be thankful for." He wiped my cheek with his thumb. "'Squito," he said. "I should have brought some bug spray."

"You can't think of everything." Had I blown it? I'd laid all the worse things about me out there for the man, why? Was I trying to drive him away? Maybe. He scared the ever-loving piss out of me. "Speaking of cooking, what did you bring us?"

He named the food as he took it out of the basket. "Smoked turkey, gouda cheese, potato salad, deviled eggs, watermelon slices, and for dessert, I made us some choco-late parfait."

"You managed all that today?"

"I made the potato salad and deviled eggs last night."

"If you thought my belching was bad, you might not like what the deviled eggs do to me."

He handed me the plate of deviled eggs and grinned. "The potato salad has hard boiled eggs too."

"You've been warned." The deviled eggs were decorated with paprika. I picked one up and ate it in a single bite. The taste of mayo, pickles, a hint of mustard, and some onion mixed with creamy hard-boiled yoke did a dance on my taste buds. I raised my brow at Brady. "You are playing with fire."

"I like fire." He leaned over and kissed me. His tongue swiped the corner of my mouth. "Yep," he said. "Them's good eggs."

"They certainly are." Every bit of the meal was delicious.

When we finished our plates and started in on the chocolate parfait, Brady said, "As you can see, I don't need someone who cooks. I'm not trying to make you into a happy homemaker if that's what you're worried about."

"I'm not worried," I lied.

"Sure," he said. "I know what it looks like when a wild animal wants to bolt. I've seen it enough in the mirror. I'm not looking to domesticate you, either. I like you, Willy."

"I like you, too."

"Then it doesn't have to be more complicated than that."

I took a bite of the parfait. It was what I imagined Heaven might taste like if you could cut a slice and put it in a spoon. "Keep feeding me like this, and I might have to marry you," I said dreamily. I heard Brady's spoon clink then realized what I'd said. "I didn't mean that like it sounded."

Brady, who'd been putting empty plates and containers in the basket as we finished each part of the meal, took my parfait.

"Hey," I pouted. I guess dinner had concluded. "Can I have that wrapped up to go?"

The sun dipped just below the horizon, and the fire cast a warm glow on Brady's gorgeous and serious face. I was usually good at reading people. Liar, not a liar. Innocent, guilty. That kind of thing. But I could not read what was going on in Brady's head right then. All I could think about was all those women who had relentlessly pursued my dad, and how he'd persistently ran away. I didn't want Brady to run.

"I'm sorry," I sputtered. "I didn't mean it, okay. We're good. No worries. I'm not trying to trap you or anything like that."

"I don't think that, Willy." He frowned. "You make some giant leaps sometimes."

"It's my job. I'm supposed to gather all the information and guess what it all means. Usually, I'm right."

"Not this time."

"Then why so serious all of a sudden?"

"Because I feel serious about you." He leaned over and kissed me again. He tasted of spiced chocolate and buttery whipped cream. "If you haven't noticed."

"I want to hop on you like a frog wants a lily pad, but I think there is still something holding you back." I remembered Ruth's earlier epiphany. "But if I'm being honest, I'm afraid you're going to hurt me."

"If I've seemed hesitant, it's only because," he rubbed his face, "I haven't talked to Jo Jo. The boy took care of me when I should have been taking care of him. Now that we both know the truth about his mother, things have changed between us for the better. I'm worried our new found peace might end when I tell him I want to be with you."

"When? Not if?"

"When, Willy." He caressed my face, and like the cat I am, I nuzzled in. "I'm going to tell him. Since this Evelyn thing, he hasn't been around much to talk."

"You're not still afraid he's involved, are you?"

"No, not with the murder. But he's hiding something."

I pressed my lips to his palm. "Like son, like father."

"Christ, I love those freckles across your nose." He kissed the bridge of my nose. "Your apple cheeks." He kissed them next. "Your downturned lips." I moved to meet his mouth. He reached back behind my head as he deepened the kiss and tugged the pins from my loose bun. My damp hair fell about my shoulders. He brought a handful to his nose. "And these curls. Damn, woman, I could lose myself in these curls."

I rose to my knees and crawled across Brady's lap to straddle his legs. "I love this tussle of cocoa brown hair that always looks like it's three weeks past a trim." I ran my fingers through his hair and scooted forward in his lap. He ran his hands up my bare thighs. I bit my lower lip then said, "I really like that, too."

He grinned.

I ran my fingers over his chest and across his broad shoulders. I remembered how he watched me tackle Roger Parks, and he didn't try to interfere or jump in. "I love the way you make me feel like a woman while treating me like an equal." I reached down and pulled up my camisole top and tugged it over my head. Surprise, well, probably not. No bra. Brady's eyes went as wide as saucers. "I love that look on your face right now while you see my body for the first time."

His hands went to my hips, my bare waist, and slid up to cup my breasts. He graze my nipple with his thumb. "Yeah, that too," I said breathlessly.

Brady pulled his T-shirt off, which would have been my next move. Thank God, he beat me to it. He had a fine dusting of dark hair across the top of his chest and a heart-break trail down the center of his stomach that kept going past the button on his jeans.

His hands slid to my back, his fingers kneading my muscles I raised up and kissed him, loving the feel of our bare chests touching. Brady held me close with one arm as he lifted me over his lap and laid me down so that my back was on the blanket and he was on top of me. I wrapped my legs around his waist, pressing against the hard erection in his jeans.

Warmth gathered at my groin, and it wasn't just the hot July heat. Holy smokes, Brady made me vibrate. Sex, in the past, had always been about the destination, but this man was taking me on a slow journey, and I didn't want it to end. He cupped my breast again, his mouth moving to my neck, my collar, my chest, until his mouth covered my nipple. I arched my back and groaned. When Brady looked up at me, his eyes had turned a brighter shade of amber, almost gold. He licked his lips, and I saw his canines had become longer, more pointed, more coyote.

"It's been a long time," he said, his voice low and hoarse with lust.

I reached for his hair and ran my claws along his scalp. He wasn't the only one losing control. I moaned again as he sucked my nipple between his lips, his teeth grazing my skin, but not breaking it. He moved against me, his groin rubbing against mine, pushing the seam of my jean shorts against my sweet spot. The familiar tingle and pressure of a building orgasm had me hooking my calf behind his legs, urging him to quicken his pace. My hands in his hair, I begged him to suck me harder. His growls of pure animal lust drove me home as I climaxed, my moans of pleasure quieting the crickets and tree frogs.

I shuddered to a finish and threw my hands to the blanket. I laughed. The pure joy of the moment burbled up out of me in an uncontrollable way. Brady dropped to his elbow and joined me. We both laughed like it was something we hadn't done in a very long time.

When we finally got control, Brady gazed down at me, suddenly serious again. His teeth were still out. *The better to eat me*, I thought. He rubbed himself between my legs again the feel of his erection sharpened the edge the first climax had dulled. "I want you, Willy. Goddamn, I want you so bad, I ache."

"Then have me," I said, my eyes watering with my need. "Have me. I'm yours."

"Yes," he said kissing my tears. "And I'm yours."

I hadn't realized that my sharp kitty fangs had come out until I cut my tongue on them. When Brady's tongue darted in my mouth, his chest rumbled at the taste of my blood. He held himself up as he undid the button and zipper on my shorts and between his hands and my feet we got both the shorts and my underwear off. I wanted him inside me as bad as he wanted to be there, and when his jeans were around his thighs, I reached between his legs and put him inside me.

He slid the rest of the way in, his thickness filling me with so much love and passion that I cried out with joy, with pleasure. He stroked into me over and over until the friction between us ripened the fruit of our lovemaking.

I ran my claws across his back. Brady reached under my arms and gripped my shoulders, holding me in place as his thrusts became more urgent. He opened his eyes, his golden gaze wild with abandon. He howled. The warmth of ecstasy eroded my senses. I screamed, "Yes!" bucking against him as my second orgasm stripped away my inhibitions leaving nothing between us but raw emotion and unrestrained bliss. Brady cried out, a moan poured from his lips, and he finally let go, thrusting once, then again, and holding us joined until he was completely spent.

This time when we collapsed, neither of us laughed. Brady held me while I cried. At one point, I stroked his cheeks, and I swear he'd shed his own tears. I felt safe. Cared for. Content.

After a few minutes, he murmured in my ear, "Are you purring?"

My eyes widened. Yep. Sure enough. "That's new."

"I like it," he said, stroking my damp curls from my sweaty face. He kissed me. "I don't want to lose you, Willy."

"I don't want to be lost."

A sudden shout of surprise brought us both up quick. I gather the blanket to my chest wishing I had my gun. Getting attacked with your pants down seemed wholly unfair. Brady struggled to get his jeans up over his thighs.

"Who's there?" I called out. The light of the fire made it difficult for my bobcat eyes to see our intruder.

"It's me," the voice said. "Jo Jo."

"Oh, dear God," I croaked. "Shit, fuck."

"I don't need a play by play," Jo Jo said.

Brady, who'd finally got his pants on, stood up. "What in blazes are you doing out here?"

"I needed to run." He walked down closer after I wrapped the blanket completely around me. "It looks like I'm not the only one."

The boy had a lopsided grin on his face. I grabbed a nearby broken twig and chucked it at him.

He dodged it easily.

"I'm sorry, Jo Jo. I didn't mean for you to find out about Willy like this. I should have talked to you sooner."

Jo Jo raised his hands. "Hey, I'm glad you finally made your move. Willy doesn't seem like the kind of woman who likes to wait."

"Excuse me," I said. "I'd wait as long as it took for your dad."

The young man gave me an appraising look. "Good answer." To his dad, he said, "Since this place is occupied. I'll go find someplace else to work off some energy."

"You don't mind?" Brady said.

"Be happy, Dad."

"I am."

Those two words made my heart do flips. "I am, too, if anyone cares."

"He cares," Jo Jo said. "See you all later."

"Bye, now. Call ahead next time," I said.

I heard Jo Jo chuckling as he walked into the woods.

"Where'd he come from?"

"The house I guess."

"It took a gazillion hours to get here, your house isn't that far from town."

Brady reached down and scooped me up, blanket and all, in his arms. "This is the property attached to the back of ours. I bought it after Rose Ann disappeared. It's an easy walk from the house, or a long scenic drive if you know the way." He smiled. "How about we check out the cabin? I changed the sheets today and everything."

"Ohhh, clean sheets. I love the way you spoil me."

He swept me inside and spent the rest of the night spoiling me for other men.

CHAPTER EIGHTEEN

*T*he next day, **Brady** and I dabbed anti-itch medicine on all of our mosquito bites. Brady had a big red bump on his ass. I guess that's what happens when you climb on top. Better him than me, because I was feeling antsy enough without an itchy butt. I'd rather spend the morning with Brady than start my day meeting with Stenson and the leaders of Peculiar.

Brady got me back to Ruth's before seven a.m. He walked me to the door and gave me a proper kiss goodbye, making me want to take him upstairs and let him spoil me some more. However, there was no way I was having sex in Ruth's house, let alone in her daughter's bed, because even I had enough manners to know that was just wrong.

Ruth and Ed were already awake, of course. They both greeted me with knowing smiles as I walked in. "Morning," I said as I passed by the kitchen.

By eight-thirty, I had showered, and I brushed my teeth, dressed appropriately, and was out the door.

Halfway to the courthouse, I remembered I'd left the backpack at Ruth's. Again. Crap. I'd have to go back for it later.

Stenson waited for me just inside the main doors. Air conditioning and all. The two of us walked into a somber room. Babel Trimmel sat behind his desk, Billy Bob leaned against the wall on the right side of the room, and Sid sat in one of the guest chairs.

"I'm sorry about why we had to send Willy to Peculiar, Babel," said Stenson after the initial greetings. I inwardly groaned. I'm sure Sunny had told Babe, Billy Bob was already in the loop, but Sid had been in the dark. "I'm not sure who reported your wife, but Willy assures me that Sunny is exactly who she appears to be." He offered an insincere smile. "Some people just like to stir up trouble."

"Especially anonymous ones." Babe, who looked a little like Karl Urban, crossed his arms and stared at Stenson. "I can't believe there was ever any doubt about my wife."

"Me, either," Sid said. His disappointed gaze met mine. I would apologize later.

"President Stenson, while it's nice to see you again after the stress of last year's Tri-State Council meeting, I have a medical practice," said Billy Bob. "My patients start stacking up about now."

"Yes, you're right, I don't want to keep you. I just wanted to make you all aware of why I asked Willy to step into the investigation of Evelyn Meyers' death."

"I'd sure like to know," Sid said his irritation evident. Yikes. I'd have to add a bottle of bourbon to go with my apology.

"Ms. Meyers was providing the council with intel on a fraud ring that has been plaguing therianthrope communities in the Tri-State area. We've been coordinating with our therian faction in the FBI since the fraud crosses state lines, and we think the people behind it have scammed human victims as well."

"Did you know about this, too, Willy?" asked Sid.

"Nope."

"Willy polices therians as directed by the Council. She wouldn't be involved with an investigation like money scams. However, since we now believe Ms. Meyers' murder is directly related to the scammers, things have changed. It's important to find the killer and bring him to a swift therianthrope justice."

In other words, Richard Stenson wanted the murderer dead, do not pass go, do not collect two-hundred dollars. Brady said he'd seen the president coming out of Evelyn's house at six in the morning. Had he been there for business or pleasure? I'd ask, but not in front of the Peculiar Trinity.

Babe stood up. "Who was Evelyn investigating?"

"She wouldn't say. Not until she had proof. She said she didn't want to ruin someone if they were innocent."

Babe sneered. "That would be a first. That woman took great pride in making folks miserable."

I'd seen the same thing just in the short few minutes I'd been around her. "It had to be someone she had a personal connection to. A close friend, maybe."

"She didn't have any close friends," Sid said.

I shrugged. "A lover then."

Babe laughed. Even Billy Bob looked amused. Sid scowled, and Stenson blanched.

Sid leveled his gaze on me. "I doubt she had a lover. Evelyn had a cold streak that damn near ran to heartless."

"I found a half empty box of condoms that begs to differ with you," I said.

All the men in the room gaped at me.

Sid shook his head. "There wasn't mention of that in any police report."

"The box was under her feminine hygiene wipes. All your deputies are men. I'm sure Connelly, who is a decent policeman, didn't touch them. Most guys wouldn't. It's like tampons and douches. You all know they exist, but you want to pretend they don't."

Sid held up his hand. "Fair enough." To Stenson, he asked, "What kind of proof was she offering?"

Stenson sat in the other guest chair, his thin face pinched. "She said she saw an accounts book, and she was certain it was the key."

Crap. That meant the ledger I found might not be Evelyn's. Which means, she wasn't a gazillionaire. Maybe. Probably. Why else would someone take it? Damn it. Now I had to come clean about my find. "I saw the book. The accounting log."

"What? Why didn't you say something?" Stenson blustered. "This could be a turning point in finding the culprit."

The sheriff was conspicuously quiet.

"I didn't tell you because I thought it listed Evelyn's

accounts, not those of a fraud ring I didn't know about until last night."

Stenson's glower lessened a smidge. "Where's the ledger now?"

"Gone," I admitted. "I saw it when I did my first unofficial sweep of Evelyn's house." I sent an apologetic look to Sid, but he was staring down at his shoes. Huh. "When I saw it hadn't been logged in the police report, I returned to the house with Deputy Farraday, and it was missing." Now that the cat was out of the bag—the cat being me—I could spill the rest. "I took pictures of the pages."

"During that unofficial visit?" asked Babel. "Which means whatever evidence you uncovered is inadmissible."

Babe's years as an integrator were shining through. Stenson said what I was thinking. "If we were planning on trying the culprit in a human court that would matter, Mayor Trimmel. But this particular case will be met with therianthrope justice."

Sid cleared his throat. "I have the book."

I think Babe and Billy Bob were as shocked as Stenson and me. "Why?" I asked. "Why take it? Why not log it into evidence?"

"To protect Jean. Evelyn spent her entire adult life making my wife miserable. I wasn't about to let her do it in death, too."

So Sid had looked through the ledger and learned enough to believe the information could harm his family. Or maybe he'd really taken the book to protect himself. I hated that Sid was a suspect, but he'd put himself on the chopping block.

Stenson had obviously reached the same conclusion. "Sheriff Taylor, you've withheld key information that could shed light on a major case, not to mention a local murder. I'll be talking to the board this afternoon about your transgression." The opossum shifter looked exasperated. "Why didn't you just give it to your daughter Nicole?"

Sid startled. "Why would I have given it to her?"

"Because she's on the fraud task force we have inside the FBI."

The hurt and confused expression on the sheriff's face told me he'd had no idea. I began to suspect that Nicole got the ledger, and Sid found it. He'd tried to protect his daughter, not his wife. Either way, it didn't bode well for the guy.

Like human towns, the sheriff's position was an elected one, just like the mayor. But unlike human communities, those in elected positions were under the purview of the Tri-State Council. Which meant, Sid could be fired. That was the last thing I wanted.

"Let's not be hasty here," Babe said. "Sid is a respected member in this town."

"And Evelyn told me it was someone well-respected in town who was behind the scams," Stenson countered.

"No one would ask Evelyn for the time of day, much less for her opinion about one of our citizens," said Babe. "The only person she thought highly of was herself."

"She didn't give you any names or real proof, either," added Billy Bob.

"And yet, she was right," responded Stenson.

"Sid Taylor is not some con artist." Billy Bob shook his head. "This is ridiculous."

"Your opinion is noted," said Stenson. "After the Council makes a ruling, I'll let you know." He nodded toward the door. "Walk me out, Willy."

He was the boss, and not just of me. Babe and Sid had to take his orders, too. I turned and followed him out of the office.

When we were out of earshot of the others, Stenson said, "I'll return to the city this afternoon. I'll call you with our decision, and you can inform the mayor."

Awesome. I'd get to be the one to deliver the bad news. "I doubt Sheriff Taylor had anything to do with Evelyn's death or with the scam. His home is modest. He and his wife don't live above their means. He's a decent guy, President Stenson."

"He let his personal feelings interfere with his investigation. A professional would have recused himself."

Pot meet kettle. Stenson's indignation was hypocritical, and I couldn't help but bristle. "Are you going to recuse yourself?" I asked. "Because you had a personal relationship with Evelyn Meyers, too."

Stenson puffed up, his mustache twitching. "I don't know what you mean."

"Maybe you want to think about your answer, sir. Surely the Tri-State Council President wouldn't lie to the lead investigator in this case."

Stenson flushed. His mouth flopped open, but no words came out.

"Two weeks ago, in the early morning, a witness saw a

man fitting your description leaving Ms. Meyer's home." I wondered if I was signing my own pink slip by pressing Stenson so hard. But if he was going to spout on about Sid's poor judgment, he had to abide by the same moral criteria. Well, I wasn't one to half-ass anything. "Your mustache is a unique feature."

He caved. "I've been seeing Evelyn occasionally since last June. Nothing serious."

Obviously. The man didn't seem too broken up about her death. "So, her suspicions were conveyed over pillow talk and not by letter."

"I told her to write the letter," he admitted. "So that I could use it to start an official investigation."

"And the anonymous communiqué about Sunny?"

"I honestly didn't know that she sent the letter about Mrs. Trimmel. I only found out when you told me last night. Evelyn only informed me about the one letter."

I believed him. Evelyn had not wanted anyone to know she pointed the finger at Sunny. Just more evidence of her vindictive behavior. I wished I could feel worse about her death. I wasn't ready to pin a medal on her murderer's chest, but I could almost understand the impulse to kill her.

"Will you admit your relationship with Evelyn to the Council?" I asked.

"It won't matter," he said. "I had nothing to do with her murder, and I can prove I wasn't in town the day it happened. Revealing information about my sex life will only muddle the waters."

Which meant he wasn't going to tell the Council jack

shit. And knowing Stenson, he'd manipulate the situation into a win. And if I came forward with the information, I'd walk away without a job. Or worse. Did I mention how much I hate therian politics?

"Take your own personal connection to this case into account when it's time to decide Sid's fate."

He nodded. "I will."

"That's all I can ask."

He gave me an appraising look. "You really are a good investigator, Ms. Boden."

I winked. "I get lucky sometimes." Like last night. God, how I'd hated leaving that awful, wonderful lumpy twin bed this morning. I watched Stenson get into his car and drive away. Fucking hell, today was already a shit show, and it wasn't even 10 a.m. I returned to Babe's office. I wanted to check in with Sid and make sure we were okay. The locals weren't the only ones who respected the sheriff. I also understood how a personal connection could blind you. If Jo Jo or Brady had been involved, I would have helped them bury the bodies. Well, maybe not that far, but I certainly wouldn't have turned them in.

Sid had already left. Babe and Billy Bob were in the middle of a serious discussion though. I knocked to let them know I'd come back. "I missed the sheriff, huh?"

"He went out the back when y'all scurried out," the doc said.

Ouch. I guess Billy Bob wasn't thrilled with me. I couldn't blame him. I didn't like me much right now, either. The last thing I wanted was to be the catalyst for Peculiar's implosion.

"I appreciate you keeping Sunny's secret, Willy," Babe said. His expression was less gratitude and more growl-itude.

"But?"

"But it doesn't change the fact that I'm furious about President Stenson riding roughshod over Sheriff Taylor. You've been in the middle of this mess from the very beginning."

"I took an oath, Brady, just like you did when you took office. And part of that oath was to do my job to the best of my ability." I blew out a breath. "Better me than an investigator who doesn't bother working with local law enforcement, much less attempt community outreach. I've worked with Sid. I like the man. I don't want to make things worse for him. Let me do my job. If I find the real killer, Sid is in the clear." At least I hoped he would be.

Babe sat down in his chair. I swore he looked older than he did last year, which is strange for our kind since we aged much slower than humans. I guess running a town, having to hide a human wife, and chase after two kids could take its toll, even on a young man.

"Okay," he said. "I won't interfere. For now."

"That's all I ask." I turned my attention to the doc. "Did you get the toxicology reports back?"

"Yes," he said. "I dropped them off at the Sheriff's Department this morning. Evelyn was definitely poisoned. She tested positive for potassium cyanide."

"Can that happen from car exhaust?"

"No. It wasn't in gas form. Her lungs would have been wetter, and she would have tested positive for hydrogen cyanide instead. She definitely ingested the poison. Not enough to kill her quickly, but she would have only lived for two to four hours before she expired. I suppose she wasn't dying fast enough for the killer, so they finished her off with the sword."

"If that's the case, it might negate the idea that the killer wanted her to suffer. It could indicate that the poisoner didn't know enough to give her the right dose for immediate death."

"Or maybe the killer did want her to suffer, and something else forced him or her to speed things up," said Billy Bob.

"I have to re-check alibis to account for the time difference. I need to know where everyone was before rehearsals."

"Oh, another thing." Billy Bob pressed his lips together and glanced around the room uneasily. "I had another patient who tested positive for cyanide. Only in a much lower quantity. Not enough to kill, just enough to cause illness."

"Who?"

"I can't tell you that. Doctor-Patient confidentiality. But after Evelyn, I am more acutely aware of the symptoms. Otherwise, I wouldn't have checked."

"I don't want you breaking patient privilege." Time to play the guessing game. "Can you tell me the symptoms of a mild case of cyanide poisoning?"

He nodded. "Headaches, fatigue, mild confusion, dizziness, anxiety."

"Thanks, Billy Bob."

His silver eyes studied me as if he'd just made up his mind. "I appreciate you not pressing me for more information."

"Would it have done me any good?"

"Nope."

"That's why I didn't press you. A good investigator knows how to read people." And besides, based on the symptoms, I was pretty sure I knew which patient had been exposed.

It was time to see a mother about her son.

CHAPTER NINETEEN

I **found out that Sabrina** Miller worked at Babcock Jewelry in Osage Beach. It was a good forty-minute highway drive from Peculiar. I imagined there were more than a few locals who found work in the neighboring human towns, even a place as small as Peculiar could only sustain so many employment opportunities. I called Brady to see if he wanted to take a ride with me.

He said, "Yes," and I did a happy dance. Yay! I got to do the two things in the world I liked the most. Investigate and hang with Brady. Also, I called Ruth to let her know where I was going. I felt bad about not inviting her along, but she let me off the hook by saying she and Ed had three cars in the shop today, but she'd see me for dinner this afternoon. I'd never had a friend like Ruth. Her strength resonated with me. Frankly, Ruth Thompson was the toughest and strongest person, man or woman, I'd ever met. I needed her in my life almost as much as I needed Brady.

I drove out to Brady's house to pick him up. I let him drive my pickup, not because he was "the man" but because I wanted to touch him, and I found it difficult to grope and steer at the same time. In other news, Brady sometimes found it difficult to be groped and keep the car on the road.

By the time the GPS got us to the jewelry store, Brady had a rock-hard bulge in his britches and opted to stay in the truck. I didn't think it would be possible for him to walk with that thing at full mast anyway.

An alarm *ding-donged* when I opened the door. A man in a dark suit was arranging gold chains inside a glass case. Sabrina Miller, who hadn't looked up, was spraying another case with glass cleaner. She had the bottle in one hand and a paper towel in the other. When the man saw me, his face brightened.

"Good morning," he said. "How can I help you? Are you looking for a gift? Something for yourself?"

"Actually, I'm here to see Sabrina."

That got her attention. She snapped her gaze to me, a curious expression on her face. "Oh, hello. You're Ruth's friend, right?" She frowned. Why do you need to see me?"

I forgot the only context she knew me in was as Ruth's friend and a patient of Doctor Smith's. Did I clue her in about my purpose or take advantage of her ignorance? Duh. Advantage, Willy Boden.

"I came into town today with my boyfriend, and I remember you told me you worked here."

"I don't remember telling you where I--" She shook her

head. "Never mind, I probably did. I was half out of my mind that day."

"I bet. A sick child is the worst." I imagined, anyhow. "How's Josh doing?"

"He's still having headaches, but he's much better."

"Did you find out what made him sick?"

She shrugged. "He's sixteen. He eats enough junk to keep Hostess in business."

"Mrs. Miller, your friend will either have to buy something or visit you another time," her boss said. His face was all pinched like he smelled something bad. I bet he was a real joy to work with day in and day out.

I pulled out my wallet and gestured to Brady sitting in the truck out front. "I think I want to buy my beau something purty."

Her boss looked annoyed, but he backed off. I stared at him until he decided to go in the back and do something else.

"So," I said to Sabrina, "I saw Josh yesterday over on Holden. I think he was with that Roger Parks, the one dating Michele Thompson. He looked much better." At least he wasn't so sick he couldn't outrun me. Talk about embarrassing. Though, if he hadn't thrown the bag over the fence, I would have totally caught him. As Brady learned last night, I am long on stamina.

Sabrina stepped back and turned to another jewelry case. "Are you looking for anything specific? A tie bar? Cufflinks? A ring?"

"Not a ring," I said too quickly. "I mean, we aren't even close to exchanging rings. Still in the early stages."

"Don't let the good times, fool you, honey. Men are pricks. Clay was big on fun, but small on responsibility."

"Brady's not Clay."

She shrugged. "I'm just being honest." I could see the barest hint of a smile grace her lips. Sabrina had enjoyed that moment of superiority. Maybe she and Evelyn had more in common than I originally supposed.

Advantage over. I opened my wallet and flashed my official Tri-State Council badge. In a barely audible whisper, I asked, "Do you know what this means?"

She nodded, fear replacing smugness in her eyes.

"Why was your son carrying a bag full of spooled chains?"

She gave her head a vigorous shake. Her boss returned to a nearby counter and moved us further across the store to stay out of earshot. "Not here," she hissed. "Tonight. I'll text you when I get off work. But if you want information from me, leave now. I need this job."

For a split second, I felt shitty. This woman had very little, and I'm sure she thought I was about to leave her with even less. But right now, I needed her scared and cooperative. "If you don't text me, I will hunt you and your son down, and we'll spend quality time at the Sheriff's office." I tilted my head until she made eye contact with me. "Understand?"

"Yes," she said. Her expression was all fear. Good. I'd made my point.

"See you tonight." I walked to the case displaying necklaces. There was a variety of gold and silver, various designs and lengths. I saw one that was mini hearts that were looped together to form a chain. It was delicate and pretty. "How much for this one?" I asked the jeweler.

"Ah, lovely little piece. It's fourteen-karat gold with a ten-karat gold clasp. Seventy-five dollars and eighty-nine cents."

"How does someone tell if it's fourteen-karat gold?" I'd never been a big jewelry person, so I was curious.

"There is a stamp." He pulled the chain out and took some kind of round magnifier from his pocket. He put his on the first heart in the chain. "Look here. You see the stamp?"

I saw the number .585. "I see it."

"It means it is fifty-eight-point-five percent pure gold. In other words, fourteen-karat. Twenty-four-karat gold would have a one-point-zero-zero-zero mark on it, meaning it's one-hundred percent pure. The closer to that number, the purer the gold. The further away, the less pure."

"Cool. I learn something new every day." He gave me an odd look. I shrugged. "It's something my dad used to say all the time." I handed him the necklace. "Wrap this up for me. Give Sabrina the commission. She was hugely helpful." And I hoped she'd be even more helpful when we met later.

BRADY TOOK me for brunch at the Sunrise Diner on the strip in Osage Beach. After, we drove down by the lake. I wasn't in a hurry to get back to the sheriff's station. By now, all the deputies would know that the Council was deciding what to do about Sheriff Taylor. They would blame me. I mean, if I was them, I would totally blame me.

Eventually, though, the call came.

And that phone call, that shitty, shitty phone call, was the reason I had to return to Peculiar.

So I could ask Sid Taylor for his badge and gun.

CHAPTER TWENTY

*P*resent time...

In ancient times, there was a reason messengers were killed. If you can't blame the one responsible, then blame the one you're with—and gut 'em with a sword.

And that's how I felt. Gutted. I hadn't gotten much sleep the night before, obviously, and I'd had to do my goddamned duty and remove a good man from his post. I was the messenger, and I would bear the brunt of the fallout in this town. And Stenson had left me out to dry. So much for relying on his conscience and doing the right thing. No wonder he and Evelyn connected; they were cut from the same cloth.

I didn't want to move Sid's gun or badge from the desk. Not now, not ever. But as long as I was an officer of the Council, I had to do as they told me. I waited until Nicole and Jean left the station with Sid.

As I reached for the items on Sid's desk, Tyler

Thompson put his badge right next to them. My heart dropped. I looked at him. "Tyler..."

Ruth came up behind him and flicked him in the back of the head. "You better pick that back up, mister."

"I'm not going to work for Willy after she got Sheriff Taylor in trouble," he protested.

"She did not get Sid in trouble. He did that all to himself." She looked at Connelly and Farraday, including them in on the conversation. "And if either of you even think about pulling the same stupid stunt, you can forget it. I love Sid as much as you do. I've spent my entire adult life with him as Sheriff, and I've known him since I was a child. If I'm not mad at Willy, then that should tell you something."

"She fought with President Stenson," Brady said. I gave him a *you-weren't-supposed-to-hear-that* look. He shrugged. "You should've walked further away if you didn't want me to listen in."

I'd gotten the call when we'd walked down to the lake in Osage Beach. I thought I'd put enough distance between us so he couldn't hear the conversation, but I guess coyotes had better hearing than bobcats.

Brady clenched his fist. "Stenson wanted to remove Sheriff Taylor permanently." He let his revelation sink in for a minute. "Willy told them she would quit if they fired Sid. She's the only reason he's only suspended. So instead of blaming her for what's happening, you should be kissing her ass and helping her solve this case so he can come back to a job he's lucky to still have."

I had to fight back a choking sob. Emotions were

tricky bitches. You could add overwhelmingly in love with the gorgeous man vigorously coming to my defense to the list of things I was feeling.

"Damn straight," Ruth said. She crossed her arms in front of her chest and dared the room to say anything different.

Like a scolded child, Deputy Thompson picked up his badge. "Sorry, Willy. I sometimes jump to conclusions too quickly." He glanced at Sunny.

She smirked. "Chavvah and I need to get back to the Outlook. Lunch crowd might have thinned, but the dinner crowd is going to be coming in soon. Kyle is a decent cook, but I'm not ready to hand the dinner prep over to him."

I stopped Sunny before she could leave. "Can I talk to you real quick?"

"Sure," she said. "But I can't help you the way you think."

"Why did you call everyone down here? What was it all for?"

My friend took my hand. "I called Babe, Chav, Billy Bob, Jean, and Nicole for Sheriff Taylor. He needed to know he had friends in the community who cared about him and had his back. I called Ruth down here for you because I didn't see the Council, I saw you. And I wanted to make sure you had someone here who had your back." She looked over my shoulder at Brady and smiled. "What I didn't foresee was that you would bring along your own knight in slightly tarnished, but still shiny armor." She let go of my hand. "I told you I was a bad psychic."

"You're pretty terrific in my book. Still no visions of whodunnit, though?"

"Nope, sorry. But I'll call you if anything pops up."

Babe, Chav, and Billy Bob all left after a few polite goodbyes, leaving me with my best friend, the man I adored, and three determined deputies.

"I don't think they'll give you any more grief," Ruth said.

"Not if they don't want you bringing the hammer down." I winked. "You're pretty bad ass, Ruth Thompson."

"Takes one to know one." She jerked her thumb toward the door. "I better get back to Doe Run. I wasn't lying this morning about being swamped with jobs. It's a good problem to have."

"See you later."

"Dinner," she said.

"I'll be there."

"You, too, Brady. I know Ed would love to see you again."

Brady gave her a crooked smile. "Sure."

Almost as if it were an afterthought, she added, "And bring Jo Jo if he's not busy." While Ruth might stay out of her children's love lives, I knew she wasn't above giving them tiny pushes.

He nodded. "I'll ask."

"Great." She gave me a quick hug and kissed Brady's cheek. "See you both later."

Unabashedly, I looped my hands behind Brady's neck and pulled him down for a kiss. "You are super awesome."

He rested his forearms on my shoulders and kissed me again. "That's how I roll."

"I recall how you roll," I told him. "I tend to remember things I'm interested in, and make no mistake, Brady Corman, I'm interested in you."

Gazing up at his face, I felt the sudden need to sing Celine Dion ballads. Jesus H. Christ, no wonder greeting card companies made so much freaking money.

A clearing of throats reminded me we weren't alone.

"Uh, hello," I said to Connelly, Thompson, and Farraday.

"Awaiting our instructions," Farraday said.

I balled my hands into fists and put his on my hips. "Okay, boys, Operation Find Evelyn's Killer and Shut Down a Fraud Ring, aka Get Sid His Job Back shall now commence. You with me?"

They all spoke their agreement.

"Great." I bared my teeth in a feral grin. Then let's get crack-a-lackin'."

"You've been dying to say that, haven't you?" Brady asked.

"You betcha."

I sent Farraday to run down Roger Parks and get his alibi for the hours of two to four p.m. If he couldn't come up with a solid story, I told Eldin to bring him in. I didn't send Tyler because of his sister's relationship with the suspect. Instead, I asked Tyler to comb through the ledger with Connelly and see if the two of them could make heads or tails of the numbers. What I really needed was a forensic accountant, but hey, a tax law attorney might do.

"Would you stay here and look over the ledger with Connelly and Thompson? I know numbers are your past, but your expertise could really help my future."

He groaned and not in a fun way. "If they are open to my help, I'll do it."

Tyler said, "Yes, please. Math is not my friend."

"Thompson, why don't you come with me to the bank? You can back me up when I talk to Milo Greene again. Connelly, you assist Brady with the ledger."

"Sounds like a plan, Willy," Connelly said. He took the accounting book from Tyler's desk and put it on his. He pulled a chair around next to his and invited Brady to sit down.

"You ready to go?" I asked Tyler.

"Yep. Let's do this."

Between Ruth and Brady, they'd turned the deputies around. I could see that all of them had renewed confidence and drive to get this case solved. I would do my damnedest to live up to their expectations.

All of them. Especially Ruth and Brady's.

CHAPTER TWENTY-ONE

*S*urprise, surprise, **Milo** Greene wasn't in. According to Sally the receptionist, he'd taken a personal day for a family emergency, but she'd be happy to take a message for him. Fuck that, I thought. That bastard was going to have a real family emergency when I caught up with him.

We took one of the police SUVs. I thought it, along with a uniformed officer, would be enough to make Milo talk. That money might not belong to Evelyn, but it certainly belonged to someone, and the banker knew who. Richard Stenson wasn't the only one who warmed Evelyn's bed. That love bird on Greene's desk matched hers. It was easy to imagine. Close neighbors, his wifey off with sick parents, he's lonely, she's lonely, one thing leads to another, yada, yada.

"Well, that was a colossal waste of time," I told Tyler as he pulled out of the bank parking lot. "Head over to your mom's house next."

"Why?"

Why? Because I'd just remembered the backpack full of possible, albeit, confusing evidence. "I need to pick something up."

When we got to Ruth's, Roger's muscle car was just driving off. Ugh. "Call Farraday and let him know which direction Parks is heading."

"You got it."

I left him in the vehicle while I ran in to get the bag. I ran into Michele on the way up the stairs. She had one of those lazy, blissful smiles that people get when everything is suddenly right with their world. I hoped Roger had an alibi. He was a douche bag, but he was her douche bag. "What's up, girl?" I said.

She had her thumb sliding along a gold necklace hanging around her neck. "Roger bought it for me. Isn't it gorgeous? And it's real gold! He must have paid a small fortune for it."

"Guilt gift?" I asked because I couldn't help myself.

"No," she said defensively. She pressed the necklace against her chest. "We had a misunderstanding yesterday. He was making it up to me."

"Uh huh." Guilt gift. Definitely. "Can I look at it?"

She shook her head. "I don't want to take it off." She peered at me through narrowed eyes. "I know what you think, but Roger didn't steal it. I know he was into some bad stuff last year, but that's over now."

"He was? Like what?"

Tyler came up behind me. "He was part of thefts

around the surrounding areas. Lake Ozarks. Camdenton. He and his buddy Kyle Avery."

"They're not friends anymore," Michele said. "Besides, most of that had been Kyle's idea."

"So, Roger says," Tyler snorted. "Jesus, Sis. You're so gullible. Kyle is lucky he got away from Roger when he did. He's finally doing some honest work for a change."

"I don't think Sunny would let Kyle work in her kitchen if she thought he wasn't trustworthy," I added.

"As in, Roger's not?" Michele huffed. She took off her necklace and handed it to me. "Fine. Take it. It'll only prove what I already know."

That Roger Parks is a lying piece of shit. I took the jewelry from her. "I'm sure it will." As I turned the chain in my hand, I saw a .999 on the clasp. That was a mark for twenty-four-karat gold, but the jeweler had said it was rare for fine jewelry to be made with pure gold. It was too soft and would be easily damaged. I put the end between my teeth.

"Hey!" Michele shouted. Tyler grabbed her hand before she could try and snatch the chain from me. "You're going to ruin it."

I bit down. It was hard as a rock. Twenty-four-karat gold would have dented from the force of my bite. "I hate to break it to you, but this isn't real gold, no matter what the stamp says. Someone sold Roger a peach but gave him a lemon."

"What?" She took the necklace back and bit down on it. "Ow." Her mood curdled. "Well, shit."

"Watch your language," Tyler said.

It was a good thing he wasn't my big brother because he'd be scolding me all the time. I looked at the piece of fake jewelry again. "That's a herringbone design, right?"

"I think so. That's what Roger said."

Crap, it had been right in front of me the whole time. "Fuck me running."

Tyler glared at me then at his sister.

"Sorry," I said, "but I think I've figured out what the fraud scheme is." I pointed to the necklace. "It's a gold scam."

I pushed past Michele and ran up to Dakota's room to retrieve the backpack. I stood there for a minute, dumbfounded, then yelled out the door. "Did Roger come upstairs to the second floor?"

Michele and Tyler came up and stood in the doorway. Michele said, "Yes, why?"

"Fuc...dge." My dirty clothes were still in a pile on the floor where I'd left them, but the coil filled bag had disappeared. "That bastard stole my evidence."

Michele sighed. "Here," she said, holding out the worthless chain. "Take it. I'm so done."

I CALLED Farraday and told him when he tracked down Roger to make sure he grabbed the backpack too. Back at the station, Connelly and Brady were still going over the books. Brady had a lot of chicken scratch written up on the blackboard. It reminded me of being back in school. Only, I'd never been this hot for teacher.

I called Babcock Jewelry in Osage Beach. Sabrina's boss answered the phone. "Hello. This is Deputy Boden of the Peculiar Sheriff's Office." Tyler raised his brow at me, and I shrugged. I didn't think special investigator the Tri-State Council would hold much weight for a human. "I have a case involving fake jewelry and wondered if you would help me with a few questions."

"Certainly, Deputy Boden. I'm happy to help law enforcement."

"Great. I have a necklace in my possession. It's a herringbone design, and it has a point-nine-nine-nine stamped in the clasp, but I tested it, and the metal in the chain doesn't indent when I bite it. I know that's not conclusive, but I've heard," *from you*, "that fine jewelry is rarely made with pure gold."

"It sounds like it might be electroplated with gold and then stamped to make it appear like the real thing, Deputy."

"Electroplated? Could someone do that, say from their home, or is it something that a manufacturer would have to do?"

"With the right equipment, it can be done at home, but it's very dangerous."

"How so?"

"To electroplate metal, the piece has to be dipped in a solution of gold potassium cyanide in order for the gold to adhere."

I put him on speaker. "Say that again?"

"I said, the metal needs to be dipped potassium cyanide in order for the metal to adhere."

The station got quiet enough to hear a fly fart. "Thank you, Mister..."

"Babcock," he said. "I own the store."

"One more question. Do you do any electroplating at your store?"

"Well." He hesitated. "I don't sell electroplated jewelry in my shop, but sometimes I do special orders for people. I do it in a well-ventilated area, though. I follow all the safe practices."

"Has any of your solution gone missing?"

"Not that I'm aware of. However, I had some chain disappear this last week."

"Was it on spools?"

"Yes. It was only worth a couple of hundred dollars, so I didn't bother to report it. Is that what this is about? Have you found my rhodium chains?"

I didn't know rhodium from Adam. "Maybe. I'll call you if I get anything conclusive." I hung up. "Connelly, Thompson. I need you both out there looking for Roger Parks. Now. I'll follow in my truck."

As the two deputies hustled out, I gave Brady a flat look. "I guess we know where the cyanide came from."

CHAPTER TWENTY-TWO

*B*rady **insisted on coming** along on the manhunt, and while I wasn't the *take-your-sweetie-to-work* kind of gal, I found it hard to say no to Brady, and honestly, I didn't want to. If he wanted to ride with me, I was happy to have him.

Farraday called in. "I found Roger's car off Old Danvers road just past the north bridge. He's not inside. Do you want me to pursue into the woods?"

"No," I said. "Wait for Thompson, Connelly, and me to get there first. We'll do a grid search in shifter form. It will be quicker."

"Roger that," Eldin said. "Er. I mean, got it."

"I know what you meant. Out." I shook my head at Brady. My enthusiasm for the chase stirred my blood and accelerated my pulse.

"You're vibrating with excitement."

"Yep." I slowed down my breathing to still my shaking hands. I hadn't been on a tracker mission since the previous June, and Chavvah had most of the fun on that one. Though, truthfully, she probably hadn't considered being stalked by a serial killer a good time.

"Damn, woman. I may have to take you out and let you hunt me down later."

"Only if I get to eat you." I bared my teeth.

"I think that's my line."

I laughed. His promise of more late-night fun only added to the rush.

Connelly and Thompson had already arrived, and the three deputies were taking off their uniforms.

"Who's the most familiar with this piece of land?" I asked.

Connelly raised his hand. "I grew up a couple of miles over. I know these woods pretty well."

Brady and I began to strip. He was still yummylicious to look at, but in this situation, my therianthrope nature asserted itself. Being a shifter was like living in a nudist colony. Most of the time a body was just a body.

Brady shimmied his jeans over his thighs. Rawr! A body was just a body unless it was my hot werecoyote's body.

"Down, girl," he said in a low voice, his grin wicked. "We are definitely playing chase when this is all over."

I shivered. Oof-ta. *Get your head in the game, Willy!* "What is Roger's animal?"

Farraday answered, "He's a mountain lion."

Big cat, eh? I might be smaller, but I was willing to bet I had a lot more experience in a catfight. "Connelly, are you okay as a squirrel going into this? I wouldn't blame you if you wanted to stay hominid in this case."

His brows furrowed. "I'll be fine. I'm small but mighty."

Thompson punched his arm and laughed. "Mighty quick, you mean."

Connelly shook his head and smiled. "I'm shifting."

"Anything in the woods we should know about? Maybe a place where Roger might go?"

"There is a hunter's blind," said Connelly.

We all winced.

"A really old one," he amended. "It hasn't been used in years." He made a line with his finger moving north to south. "A stream runs through the property about a half mile in. The blind is south-west of the stream."

"Does he know we're looking for him?"

Farraday shrugged, the pupils in his gray-green eyes pinpoint for sharp focus. "I doubt it. He didn't try to hide his car."

"Good," I said. "Connelly you go north and follow the stream down. Stick high in the trees, but remember, mountain lions are climbers. Farraday, you and Thompson fan out moving east to west here in the middle of the property. Sound off if you catch his scent. Brady and I will go south and follow the stream up."

Brady nodded to me. "Be careful. Roger is scrappy."

"So am I." I didn't tell him to watch his six because I'd be doing it for him.

The freedom of the shift washed over me as fur sprouted over my skin like soft velvet against a baby's ass. As the bones shifted inside me, the magic of the change made me smaller, lighter, more agile. When I completed the change, I looked over to see a brown coyote staring at me, his tongue lolling to the side of his mouth.

That's my man. He was a gorgeous pooch. Almost like a big dog. To the right of us, sat a squirrel, a brown fox, and a twelve-point buck. I hadn't thought about Thompson being a deer. They were not predators, but deer were fast, and those antlers could do some damage if it came down to it. That's why most predators didn't hunt strong males alone. They could hold their own in a one-on-one fight.

I roared, well, more of a scream really, and we all headed off in our specified directions. Roger Parks scent was fresh, and I'd chosen the right path for myself and Brady. I smelled human not mountain lion. Roger hadn't shifted. Whatever he was doing on this property had nothing to do with the call of the wild.

I sniffed the air to let Brady know that I was on the trail. He whined and sniffed the air to show me he already knew. His amber eyes locked on me. He nudged me with his muzzle to the left, and he began to run toward the right. He wanted to circle around, each of us taking a side. I liked the way he thought.

A metal shed, probably twelve feet square sat close to where Connelly had said there was a hunting blind. I heard the whir of a fan blowing at a vent near the top of the structure. I crouched low, and I crept closer to the shed. There was a window on the door, but in my current form, I couldn't reach it without completely giving myself away.

Fuckity-fuck.

I made an executive decision and shifted back. I duck walked to the door and raised up just enough to peek inside. Roger Parks wore a white paper suit over his clothes, goggles, and a respirator mask. He had rubber gloves on that stretched up to his elbows.

We'd found the ground zero for the fraud squad. Clever. They had to know that shifters probably avoided this area like the plague. I was surprised no one had torn it down. I watched Roger pour the liquid solution into a Pyrex measuring cup. He walked toward the door. I ducked down and moved to one side.

The front door flew wide pushing me out into the open. Roger threw the cup of liquid at me. I screamed, turning my face away from the shower. "You triggered my motion sensors, bitch!"

I crashed to the ground, stunned. The liquid splashed my back, my right arm, and my legs. The solution didn't sting, but I knew my body would absorb the toxin. I got to my knees, with the intention of getting to my feet and whooping his ass.

"Get up, and I will kill you," he said. I noticed then his ashen pallor and bulging eyes. I knew fear when I saw it. Roger showed me the measuring cup and I saw that the Pyrex was only half full. His hands shook so hard, the cyanide splashed around. "Get the fuck out of here."

Roger's terror was almost palpable. Why would he be so frightened if he was in charge of the scam? No, he acted more like a lackey. I wasn't taking ass-whooping off the table, but I reversed tactics, trying a softer approach.

"You don't want to hurt me, Roger. I'm a cop. You know what happens when you kill a cop, right?"

"I get brownie points in hell." His voice trembled. I

could see in his expression he finally realized the full impact of what he'd done. "Why? Why did you come here?"

"You know why." I had to get the cyanide off my skin. Spots on my arm were already turning bright pink as my pores absorbed the poison. "Let me wash this shit off me. Then we can talk." A quick dip in the stream might be enough to stave off the cyanide's effects.

"It's too late," he murmured. "Fuck. It's too late."

I sprung to my feet and moved back. My sudden move startled Roger so much, he almost dropped the Pyrex. Unfortunately, he held on it and then stepped forward, aiming the measuring cup in my direction. "I'm sorry, Ms. Boden. I really am."

I moved back quickly. Too quickly. The back of my foot hit a thick tree root, and I went down hard. I fell against the huge trunk of the offending tree, scraping my back and possibly twisting my ankle.

Fuck this. I started to shift.

I heard Brady's snarls before he appeared, tearing around the back of the blind and straight at Roger. Fear for my man chilled my blood.

Roger turned, obviously intending to throw the cyanide on Brady.

I finished shifting quicker than I thought possible. I leaped and knocked Roger off his feet. It didn't matter if I got more cyanide on me—but I'd be damned if I allowed that punk to hurt Brady.

The Pyrex glass arced through the air, and landed a few feet away, its poisonous contents sinking into the dirt.

But my bobcat was not satisfied, and I was in sync with her demand for vengeance. I sunk my claws and teeth into Roger's right calf. He let out a surprised yelp and tried to scuttle backward. Roger kicked at me with his free leg, his booted heel punching my shoulder. I barely felt it. I wasn't letting go until Brady was safe.

Until Roger couldn't hurt him.

My fangs dug deeper into his flesh. Warm blood filled my mouth, the rusty taste coating my tongue.

"Baby, it's okay."

Brady's voice infiltrated my single-minded goal to protect him.

"Let go, Willy. Just let go."

Brady's naked human body, covered in blood, crouched next to me. His gaze was calm, his voice soft.

"Let go," Brady said again. "I need you, baby. Please let go."

With Brady whispering comfort and his big hands stroking my fur, I calmed enough to spit Roger's mangled leg out of my mouth. I shifted into my human form and immediately started shaking. My head hurt, and I felt like vomiting. "The cyanide," I said, my voice weak. "He dumped some on me."

Brady bent forward to pick me up.

"No." I hit at him. "Don't touch me. You'll get it on you."

"Fuck that." Brady scooped me up and began to run. In a few seconds, he and I were submerged in the creek. He used mud and moss and whatever was handy to wash me clean. I just prayed it wasn't too late.

CHAPTER TWENTY-THREE

I **didn't exactly feel better** after being dunked in the cold water and scrubbed with mud. Go figure, right? My symptoms seem to worsen, and I felt so dizzy. The kind of dizzy that happens right before passing out. *Don't pass out. You're a bad ass, remember?*

"Is she okay?" called out Farraday.

"She will be."

"Gotta get back to the scene," I yelled, my voice hoarse. "Not done investigating."

"The deputies are already on site," answered Farraday. He paused. "She doesn't look good, Brady. You better get her to Doc Smith quick."

"Call him," directed Brady as he lifted me into his arms and walked out of the creek. "Tell him what happened and that we're on the way."

I managed to stay awake while Brady ran all the way from the creek to my truck. He tucked me inside, and I realized we were both still naked. At least Brady had managed to wash most of the blood off him. I don't think I stayed conscious the whole time. As I drifted in and out, Brady kept a hand on my thigh.

"Please don't take her from me," I heard him say. "Please don't let her die. I can't lose her. Not her too. I can't. I won't survive it. I'm not strong enough. But if you just let her live, I'll never be weak again." When the truck stopped. He pulled me out and cradled me in his arms. "Please don't leave me, Willy. Please, please don't leave."

The next thing I knew, we were at the clinic.

Billy Bob waited for us, but Brady refused to let me go. He carried me to a room with a twin-sized bed. Billy Bob waved a noxious-smelling stick under my nose. I recognized the scent of amyl nitrate. It was also known as a popper. I roused and tried to sit up.

"No, not yet," the doc said. "Hold still, Willy."

"Is she going to be okay, Doc?" Brady asked. "Tell me she will be okay."

"I think her exposure was minimal. I'm going to run a sodium nitrate IV and give her glucose. I don't have a full cyanide antidote kit, but you did the right thing washing the excess liquids off her." He looked at Brady's arms. "Are you feeling dizzy?"

"No," Brady said then stumbled into the chair next to my bed.

"Brady!" I cried out and attempted to move toward him.

"If you don't stop wiggling, I'm going to strap you down, Willy." Billy Bob waved a popper under Brady's nose. My man sat up straighter and then reached over to hold my hand.

"I'll set up this room for two. You are both getting treated. I can help with the physical issues, but I can't do anything about your stupidity." Billy Bob shook his head. "You're lucky to be alive." On that note, he strode out of the room.

"You saved me," I told Brady.

He squeezed my hand. "As I recall, you saved me first."

I had the feeling he wasn't talking about Roger. I got angry all over again when I thought about how that boy tried to kill us. Had I imagined his fear? Maybe so. My so-called compassion must've overridden my common sense. Anyone vile enough to throw cyanide at people no doubt had what it took to poison and stab Evelyn Meyers.

"What happened to Parks?" I asked.

"Dead. Connelly flew out of a tree like a kamikaze squirrel and attacked Roger's head. It was just enough for me to take him off-balance. When he hit the ground, I tore out his throat."

Good on Connelly. Deputy Squirrel more than proved his mettle out there. "Parks deserved it." I thought briefly about Michele and felt gut-punched. No matter how I felt about Roger Parks, I still felt bad for Michele. She cared about him—and she'd grieve.

"I think he killed Evelyn," I said. "To protect his money-making scam."

"Who killed Evelyn?" asked Jo Jo as he walked into the room. He studied us, his expression a mixture of concern and fear. "Jesus, you two look like hammered crap."

"You say the nicest things, " I croaked. My throat felt so dry. Ugh. I hated being sick and stuck in a hospital. At least Brady shared my pain. We could get through anything together.

Jo Jo barked a laugh and raised his hands in mock surrender. "I give up." He eased next to the bed. "Did you really catch Evelyn's killer?"

"Roger Parks."

Jo Jo frowned. "I thought Evelyn was poisoned before rehearsal and then stabbed with the sword later."

"She was," I said. "We caught Roger red-handed with the cyanide."

"I'm no fan of Roger's, but I know he was having sex with Katrina Wells during the time the wicked witch of Peculiar was murdered." His expression turned fierce. "After rehearsals, I confronted him."

"So the blood and swollen knuckles happened because you got into a fight?" asked Brady. He sounded relieved.

"I didn't want Michele to find out about Karina," Jo Jo said. "That's why I didn't say anything. She deserves better than Roger Parks."

Farraday knocked on the open door. "Can I come in? Hey, Jo Jo."

"Thanks for calling me, Eldin."

"No, problem. I would've wanted to know if my dad and his mate were in the clinic for an emergency."

I almost corrected Eldin about the mate thing, but since Brady didn't, I kept my mouth shut. Whether it was true or not, I liked the sound of it.

Farraday held up my phone. "Your texts are blowing up.

You want to check it, or do you want me to shut your phone off?"

I said, "Gimme the phone," at the same time that Brady said, "Shut it off."

I looked at him like he'd lost his mind.

"Give her the phone," he amended.

The doc came in with four IV bags, two IV kits with dual ports, and started on me first. I checked my phone with the hand on the arm he wasn't using as a pin cushion.

"It's Sabrina. She wants to meet me at the community center tonight."

"Well, that's impossible," Brady said.

"I know." I sighed. "But if Roger didn't kill Evelyn, Sabrina is our best lead to who did."

"I can meet with her," Eldin offered.

The pieces clicked together. Holy shit. Josh. Roger. Evelyn. Babcock jewelry. All roads led to Sabrina. I smiled. "I have an idea."

"I'm not going to like it, am I?" Brady asked.

I put the phone on my lap and reached my hand out to him. "Probably not."

"Oh," Brady added. "I have a theory about the ledger. It popped into my head when I was scrubbing you down. I have no idea why."

"Rubbing my body can inspire all kinds of great ideas."

Brady grinned. "You want to hear it or not?"

"Spill."

A COOL HAND on my forearm woke me up at two in the morning. "Willy," a woman said. "Don't scream." I felt a blade against my neck. "I'm sorry. I can't tell you how sorry I am. I didn't mean to kill Evelyn. She just kept coming at me."

"Hello, Sabrina," I said. I was alone in the room, and I knew the clinic appeared empty. I was the spider, and Sabrina was the fly. "We both know Evelyn's death wasn't an accident."

The blade pressed harder against my carotid. "I never wanted to be a part of this," she hissed. She was getting more agitated. "But Evelyn left me no choice. I would have been on the streets if I hadn't agreed to do the job."

Her hands trembled. I felt a small trickle of blood run down the side of my neck. "If you put the blade down, we can talk about this. No one else needs to get hurt."

"We have to leave the clinic," she said. "I can't take a chance someone will walk in on us."

"No one's here. It's just me." I tried to make my voice sympathetic. "I know you want to unburden. You're a single mom. It can't be easy. Desperation can make the strongest person do things they never imagined they were capable of doing. Awful things."

With her free hand, Sabrina took out her phone and sent a text message.

"Did you send that to Milo?"

Her eyes widened. "How did you know?"

"He's in charge of the operation, right?"

"You're too smart for your own good. Milo was right about you being a pain-in-the-ass."

"You listen to that guy? He's the one who killed Evelyn."

"No," she said. "Evelyn was screaming at me. Ranting. I picked up the sword just to threaten her. I thought she was going to shift and attack me. Instead, she threw herself on the sword. A few minutes later, she was dead."

"So you pinned her to the wall?"

"I...I didn't mean to."

I shifted left so that the blade was no longer over a major artery. "She was already dead. Don't you get it? Milo poisoned Evelyn. He did it with the potassium cyanide you stole from the jewelry store."

Sabrina looked unsure, and I knew my words were getting to her, making her doubt Milo.

"Evelyn was hallucinating. Her brain and organs were being denied oxygen. She was already dying. If you hadn't stabbed her, she would've been dead within a few minutes." I paused to let the information sink in. "Did Milo say he'd help you? Of course, he would. Because he could use your guilt as leverage, and you would never be the wiser that he was the cold-blooded killer, not you."

"Don't listen to her, Sabrina. Ms. Boden uses people and their fears against them to get what she wants," Milo Greene said, joining us.

Finally, the puppet master. Everyone had been dancing while he pulled the strings. All his puppets took the risks, and he reaped the rewards. Now I understood why Roger was so scared. Milo wore the mask of congeniality, but it couldn't hide his true nature.

"I think you're confusing me for you. Tell Sabrina how

you went to Evelyn's in the afternoon when you found out she stole your ledger." I remembered the missing slices of cake and the ants on the deck table. "Let me guess, you two ate coffee cake out on the deck. Maybe had some tea or coffee to go with it." That would explain the twin rings created by the teacups in the sink. "At some point, you put cyanide in her cup—"

"There," Milo said. I saw he had a gun in his hand now. And his expression was all arrogance. "That's where you're wrong. I put a few drops on her piece of cake while she wasn't looking. Not enough to kill her fast. Just enough, so that I would be far away from her when she died."

He most likely wrote "Bitch" in the dust as well, but I would skip the unimportant details. "And then, Sabrina, he let you think you killed her." I cast a triumphant gaze at Milo. "Like I said."

Sabrina stumbled back from me and held the knife out, its wicked blade pointed at Milo. "You lied to me. You tricked me!"

He aimed the gun at her. Yay, all the weapons were pointed at someone else but me. Imminent death averted.

"How did you know I was involved?" Milo asked. His arrogance wouldn't let him believe anything he did contributed to his downfall. Narcissists were always the heroes of their own twisted tales. "It was Roger Parks, wasn't it? That stupid kid. It was the car, right? He wanted that goddamn car. I warned him it was too much."

"It wasn't Roger or the car, asshole. It was the accounts book. Once Brady figured out your system, the rest was a bunch of educated guesses. The biggest payouts were always to The Big Grape. And that's you. Grape for Greene. There were payouts for the last year to Plum—Parks, right? And then there were two payouts for the Mango and Little Melon. Miller and Miller. Your two newest recruits before Evelyn stole your book."

"Everything is circumstantial," said Milo, but I saw the doubt in his eyes. He swung the gun in my direction. "You can't prove anything. And I'm going to kill you, so your mouth will stay shut."

"Smile." I pointed to a tiny red light that looked like it could be part of the medical equipment. "You should look pretty for the video. I'm thinking of calling this film The Asshole Who Fell for the Oldest Trick in the Book. What do you think?"

The lights came on, blinding all of us. Three dogged deputies and one cool coyote swarmed into the room. The deputies trained their guns on the bad guys. Milo handed over his weapon. Sabrina dropped her knife.

I looked at Sabrina. "I bet if you turn witness against Milo, the Tri-Council might show you some leniency. You won't be off the hook, but you may see your son again. It's better than dying." To Milo, I said, "Your only hope of surviving this is if you give up all your partners in the three-state area. This is not a one-man show, and the Tri-Council wants it to stop."

Connelly and Farraday took Sabrina and Milo away in cuffs. Thompson grabbed the recorder for evidence and followed them out.

Brady came around the bed, his hand moving along my arms, my face, and my neck. "You're bleeding," he said.

"It's a nick. I bet you've done worse shaving."

"I can't believe how many times I nearly burst into the room. I couldn't stand watching them point weapons at you. It was a stupid risk."

"It worked." I caressed his cheek. He crawled into bed next to me on the side without the IV. "Hey, where are your bags?"

"I pulled out the line. I'm fine." He pulled me into his arms. "I can't believe it's over. I almost lost you. I can't." He buried his face in my hair. "I just...I can't."

"You won't lose me, Brady. I'm yours, and you're mine. I'm not letting you out of my sight so some other kitty can pounce in and grab you."

"You know I'm in love with you, right?"

"You've been pretty obvious about it," I teased. Inside, my heart was doing flips of joy. Brady Corman loved me. He was in love with me. This was real.

"You're the worst," he said, his lips moving against my neck.

I turned my face to his. Softly, I said, "I know. I really am the worst. Are you sure you want to be with someone like me?"

"As much as I want to breathe," he said, his words echoing the way I felt about him.

"Then it's a good thing I'm in love with you too."

CHAPTER TWENTY-FOUR

*F*our *weeks later...*

A lot had transpired since we appre-
hended Evelyn's killer and put a stop to a major fraud ring
in the Tri-State area. All-in-all, the lot of us came off
looking like rock stars. Milo Greene and Sabrina Miller
sang like canaries, and their fates are still undecided by the
council. Josh Miller was sent to live with his father Clay in
Springfield, Missouri. At least the kid will get a fresh start.
With a significant portion of the *Hamlet* cast either dead or
incarcerated, the town decided to put the play on hold for
the time being. President Stenson was so grateful to me for
the win, he agreed, reluctantly, to accept my resignation.
Sheriff Taylor on the other hand, who had been reinstated
the week after the arrests, enthusiastically accepted my
application to become a deputy for the quaint town of
Peculiar.

The sheriff was still struggling to come to terms with
the fact that his extremely intelligent daughter had

decided the best use of her degree was to work for the FBI, but it was better than him thinking she was into illegal activities. I'd finally relocated after I'd served out my notice with the Council, and Ruth had invited Brady, Jo Jo, and me over for a "Welcome Home" celebration dinner.

Considering I was staying with her for the moment, her house kind of was my home. I was betting Dakota would be glad to eventually have her room back. When Ruth said dinner, though, what she really meant was potluck, and she'd not only invited the Cormans and me, but she'd also invited half the community.

"We haven't had a potluck since Sunny moved to town," Ruth said. "Isn't this nice?"

If by nice she meant freaking awesome, then, "Yes, this is nice." I put my arm around her shoulders and pulled out a box I'd meant to give to her for more than a month.

"What's this?" She took it and turned the box in her hand. "What did you get me?"

"Just open it."

She did. Inside was the chain with all the gold hearts looped together. Ruth beamed. "You shouldn't have!"

"That smile tells me I should have."

She put it on. "How does it look?"

"Very pretty."

"Does this mean we're going steady?"

"You're making this awkward," I told her.

Ruth laughed. "Good. That's what best friends are for." She touched the necklace. "I have to go show, Ed. Maybe it will give him some ideas."

"For more jewelry?"

"Of course." And on that note, she flitted through the crowd.

Brady found me. He put his arms around me from behind and sniffed my hair. I shook my head and wiggled my butt against his upper thighs. "You know sniffing me every time you see me is weird?"

"It's weird that you like it," he said.

"True," I said. I did like it. He said I smelled like home to him, and I hoped one day I would be home for him. He crossed his arms under my boobs. The curse or the blessing of being so short. "I've got a surprise for you."

"You do?" I pressed my butt against him again. "I have a surprise for you, too."

"Which I will take great pleasure in unwrapping later, but first I want to show you something. You think we could sneak out of here for a bit?"

"I'm game." I loved the idea of sneaking off with my guy to parts unknown so we could explore our known parts.

A thirty-minute truck ride later, I recognized the small gravel road. "Hey, it's our cabin by the pond. Is this our one-month sex-aversary? Usually, I'm much better at remembering dates."

"You're nuts, woman."

"And you love it!" I countered.

We pulled in, and the log cabin was gone. Then I noticed a large pad of concrete about forty feet by forty feet. We got out of the truck. Brady took my hand and walked me over to the big slab. "What do you think?"

"I think it might get a little rough on my ass if you're planning to get me horizontal on it." I reached back and squeezed his package. "But like I said before, I'm game. And I heal fast."

"You really are nuts." He laughed. "It's the concrete pad for the house I'm building for you."

My chest squeezed, stealing my breath for a moment. "For me?"

"Well, for us. If you want?"

"What about your house?"

"It's Jo Jo's now. We can rent something until this one is built."

I turned in his arms. He had a small box in his hand. My face went numb as *oh my God, oh my God, oh my God, this is happening*! went through my head. He opened up the box. Inside was a plain platinum band.

"Willy Boden, I never want to be apart from you. Will you do me the honor of marrying a man who will never be worthy of your love, but will always cherish you until death takes us both because I'm here to tell you, when you go, I'm following you into the grave."

"What if you die first?"

"Is that a yes?"

"Brady Corman, it's about damn time you asked me to be your wife. Yes, sexy beast, I will marry you as long as you do that thing, you know, the one I like with your tongue and all."

"Yes," he said. "I promise."

"Every night?"

"Won't you get tired of the same ol'?"

"I think your tongue will get tired before I get tired of it."

He laughed. "Fair enough."

"Aren't you going to put a ring on it?" I held out my left hand.

Brady took the bright band out of the box. Inside, he showed me an inscription before slipping it on my finger. It read, *To Willy, the air I breathe.*

The End
Read the next books in the Series!

Furred Lines
(Peculiar Mysteries & Romances Book 6)

A series of murders across the state sends rookie

FBI agent Nicole Taylor to familiar territory—her hometown of Peculiar.

*****

When I am assigned my first case, a dangerous serial killer known as Little Piggy, I am thrilled and excited to put my profiler skills to the test.

I might have an advanced degree in psychology and graduated top of my class at Quantico, but my partner, the oh-so-yummy senior field agent and werebear Dominic Tartan, acts like I'm still in school.

Half the time he acts like he wants to ditch me, the other half of the time I'm pretty sure he wants to kiss me.

He's not the only one struggling. I don't know whether to sock him one or jump his bones. Most of the time I want to do both.

The case gets personal when Little Piggy takes someone from Peculiar. Dom and I need to put our differences and our hormones aside to catch the supernatural criminal before his latest kidnap victim ends up dead.

My Wolfy Wedding
Peculiar Mysteries & Romances Book 7

***Billy Bob Smith** and **Chavvah Trimmel** cordially request the honor of your presence on their happy (disastrous) day. To celebrate (survive) their union on Friday, the Twenty-First of December.*
Destination: Peculiar, Missouri.

*****

The only thing I want more than to marry Billy Bob is to have his baby, but since that ship has sailed thanks to prior trauma, I'm just happy to get him down the aisle. The date is set for the winter solstice, but a challenge from an unexpected guest is turning my special day into a fight-club nightmare.

I've already had to postpone my wedding twice, and I'm starting to think fate hates my guts.

On top of that, there are almost forty werewolves camped out on Billy Bob's property, claiming that the both of us are their new leaders. I suspect my spirit guide Brother Wolf has a hand in this new development, but he isn't taking my calls. Worst, the silent deity is sending my BFF Sunny visions that are taking a physical toll on my human friend's all too frail body.

Throw in Billy Bob's manipulative father, my pushy mother, and other surprise guests, and I'm worried we are never going to make it to "I do!"

Sense and Scent Ability
(A Nora Black Midlife Psychic Mystery Book 1)

MY NAME IS NORA BLACK, **and I'm fifty-one-years young. At least that's what I tell myself, when I'm not having hot flashes, my knees don't hurt, and I can find my reading glasses.**

I'm also the proud owner of a salon called Scents & Scentsability in the small resort town of Garden Cove, where I make a cozy living selling handmade bath and beauty products. All in all, my life's is pretty good.

Except for one little glitch...

Since my recent hysterectomy, where I died on the operating table, I've been experiencing what some might call paranormal activity. No, I don't see dead people, but quite suddenly I'm triggered by scents that, in their wake, leave behind these vividly intense memories. Sometimes they're unfocused and hazy, but there's no doubt, they are very, very real.

Know what else? They're not my memories. It seems I've lost a uterus and gained a psychic gift.

When my best friend Gilly's abusive boyfriend ends up dead after a fire, and she becomes the prime suspect, I end up a babysitter to her two teenagers while she's locked up in the clink. Add to that my super sniffer's newly acquired abilities and a rash of memories connected to the real criminal, and I find myself in a race to catch a killer before my best friend is tried for murder.

Earth Spells Are Easy
(Grimoires of a Middle-aged Witch Book 1)

As a FORTY-THREE-YEAR-OLD, newly divorced, single mom, I know two things for certain, starting over sucks, and magic isn't real. At least that's what I thought. I mean, starting over really does stink, but when it comes to magic, I have to rethink everything.

I've spent the last year since my ex left me going through the motions. Get up. Work. Care for a grumpy teenager. Cook dinner. Go to bed. Wash. Rinse. Repeat.

Nothing changes... Until it does.

After bidding on a box of old books at an estate auction, I'm experiencing changes.

And I'm not talking about menopause.

My garden gnome Linda has come to life. No, really. Her name is Linda, and she never shuts up. A chonky cat with a few secrets of his own has adopted me. And a gorgeous professor of the occult tells me I'm a witch.

Right now, I'm not sure who's crazier—me, Linda or the hottie professor.

If this is my new reality, it's nature's cruel midlife trick. I'm learning fast that earth spells might be easy, but they aren't cheap. All magic exacts a toll, and if I don't master the elements, the elements will be the death of me.

Literally.

FURRED LINES - SNEAK PEEK

Peculiar Mysteries & Romances Book 6

Chapter 1

I took a deep breath and straightened my collar. "I am an FBI agent," I said to myself in affirmation. "Special Agent Nicole Taylor and I've earned the right to be here. Nothing can take this away from me but me."

As I continued to mutter my new mantra, I assessed my outfit for the umpteenth time. I'm a therianthrope, a person who can turn into an animal. In my case, the animal is the *Procyon lotor*—you know, a raccoon. Fun fact about raccoons, their paws are extremely sensitive. Even in my human form, my hands and feet are crazy responsive. Thus... my choice of the black, riveted boots.

The stylish boots were formal enough for my black slacks, black faux-fur lined bomber jacket, and a dark blue button-down shirt, but had just enough rock-n-roll toughness to help me get away with my silver aviators. My black hair was pulled back into a severe ponytail. I wore little makeup other than some concealer under my eyes, which were naturally dark because, hel-lo, raccoon here, and a tiny bit of lip color. I checked out myself in the black sedan's side mirror and was satisfied I had successfully straddled the line of professionalism and vanity.

I noticed movement out of the corner of my eye and straightened to watch the man cross the parking lot at the Kansas City Field Office. I'd been told I would be assigned to a senior agent who had spent the past several years working undercover. I don't know what I'd expected, maybe a beard, rough hair, tattoos, and the edge of a thug. Instead, I got a man with a chiseled jawline, a perfectly aquiline nose, sharp cheekbones, firm sensuous lips, and the palest green eyes I've ever seen. I reached out to brace myself against the hood of the car, missed and tripped forward. My cute boots that had seemed like a good idea minutes before acted as a wedge when I tried to catch myself, and they sent me careening forward.

Right into Mr. Green Eyes's arms. I congratulated myself for not lingering over his bulging biceps as he assisted me into an upright position.

"Doctor Nicole Taylor?" he asked, his mouth tugged up at the corners in a wry smile. "You are Doctor Taylor, right?"

"Yes," I said when I'd swallowed enough spit to wet my dry throat. Jesus, this man was the eighty candles on my grandmother's last birthday cake. Hot, hot, hot. It was a fire I definitely needed to blow out, and no, that isn't a euphemism. This man was going to be my partner and mentor on my first big case. The bureau frowned on fraternization in the ranks, and I had no plans to jeopardize my career before it got started. "You must be Special Agent Tartan."

He looked me over, and while he seemed amused, he didn't look all that impressed. "I read your file, Doctor Taylor. You have a Ph. D. in behavioral psychology." He shook his head. "And still, you chose to go to Quantico and join the FBI instead of private practice."

I crossed my arms so I wouldn't fidget. "That's right." I made direct eye contact and didn't allow my voice to waver. "And you have a bachelor's in criminology and twelve years of field experience. And, by your half-flirting half-condescending tone, I can tell you are attracted to me, but you don't think I'm cut out for the work, so you can't decide if you want to drop me straight away or sleep with me first and then get rid of me." I smirked as he stopped smiling. "I'm here to tell you, neither will happen. I'm not a horny teenager who can't keep it in her pants, and I'm a damn good agent."

"There is more to field work than test scores," Tartan said.

"And there's more to me than what you see," I countered. I'd always been on the shorter side, so he towered over me by at least nine inches. I didn't flinch under his heated gaze.

After a few seconds, he nodded. "We'll see."

"Yep." I nodded back.

We faced off for another few seconds until Tartan pulled his coat collar up and said, "Do you have the keys? Or are we going to stand in this cold parking lot all day?"

"Oh." The heat of a blush warmed my cheeks. It was February in Missouri, and the temperature, which had been in the sixties yesterday, was in the thirties today. I dug the car keys from my pants' pocket and unlocked the door with the fob. "Where we off to?"

"Springfield," he said. "A man went missing two nights ago. We believe he is another victim of the guy the news is calling the Little Piggy killer."

Information about the serial killer taking the victim's pinky toes had been leaked to the press, and one reporter had used the nickname as clickbait to get people to read her article. It had worked, and unfortunately, the name caught on.

"No body?" I blinked in surprise. "The last three bodies have been placed near their homes within a week of going missing, right?" His M.O. had been all over the news the past six months since the third victim was found. "Do you think this guy is still alive?"

He opened the passenger side of the car. "Our job is to find out."

I frowned as he got inside and buckled up. Springfield was about two hours south of Kansas City. I got behind the wheel. "I'll take forty-nine highway to thirteen all the way down unless you want me to take a different route."

"You're driving," Tartan said. He pulled his phone wrapped with earbuds from his jacket and put the speakers in his ears. He gave me a sideways glance as he put his seat back. "Wake me when we get there."

"I'd hoped we could talk about the case on the way down."

My partner turned on some music, sort of a grungy-blues tune I'd never heard. He cranked the volume then closed his eyes.

"I guess we aren't talking about the case," I muttered.

"Good guess," he muttered back.

My eyes widened. How in the world had he heard me over all that loud music? In an even quieter voice, I said, "Looks like Clark Kent. Hears like Superman."

He took the earbuds from his ears and stared at me. "You think I look like Clark Kent?"

I actually thought he looked more like Superman, the latest Henry Cavill version, but I had been trying to provoke him. "There's no way you could have heard me. And you weren't facing me so you couldn't have read my lips. Who are you? And even more to the point, what are you?"

He put his buds back in and leaned back. "I'm your partner, for now. Dominic Tartan. A black bear therianthrope. And you're Nicole Taylor, daughter of Sid and Jean Taylor, raccoon therianthropes." He opened one eye and smirked at my expression. "I guess you don't know everything about me, do you?" He gestured with his chin. "By the way, your dad told me to tell you hi, and that you should call your mom. She worries."

I started the car, my hands shaking as I pulled out of the parking space and got on the road. Dominic Tartan, the FBI agent assigned as my partner was a shifter? And how in the hell did he know my dad? I fought the urge to scream as I headed down Summit Street and away from our field office. This. Was. Not. Happening. My dad, the sheriff of Peculiar, had somehow managed to set me up.

As if on cue, my phone rang. I pulled it out of my pocket. A picture of my mom displayed on my screen with the option of red to decline or green to answer.

"You going to ignore that?" Dominic asked.

I tapped the red circle. "Yep."

It rang again. Ugh.

"Mommy issues?"

"You have a psychology degree?"

"Nope."

"Well, I do. So how about you let me worry about me, and you worry about you." I tapped the green button and put the phone to my ear. "Hi, mom." I plastered a fake smile on my face because my mother would hear the irritation in my voice otherwise. She might not be a psychologist either, but she could read people like no one I'd ever met before, and her intuition was off the charts. "Sorry I dropped your call. I was in the middle of something."

Dominic raised his brows at me.

"It's all right, puddin'. I'm just calling to see how your first day is going?"

"Oh, fine." I tried not to sound like I swallowed a bug. "Everything is A-okay."

"Well, that's great. I'm glad to hear it."

I adjusted the phone between my shoulder and ear. "Did you need anything else, Mom?"

"Your dad says hi."

I glanced at Dominic. "That's what I hear."

The silence on Mom's end was deafening.

"I've got to go. Love you."

"Love you right back," she said and hung up.

I dropped my phone into the carrier in the car's console.

"You shouldn't drive while on the phone," Dominic said.

"Thank you for that public service announcement, Agent Tartan. My eyes have been opened, and you have changed my world. You're a hero."

A sound emitted from him that was a combination of grunt and snort. "You're welcome, *puddin'*."

One of the things I didn't miss about living in a town of therianthropes was the lack of privacy. In our human forms, we were a little stronger than humans, and our senses were more in tune with our surroundings. In other words, Dominic, as a werebear, who could hear my whispers over his loud music, had also listened to every word my mom had said to me. "Why was I assigned to you, Agent Tartan?"

"Call me, Dom." He scrolled through some files on his tablet.

I gripped the steering wheel tight enough to turn my knuckles white. "That's not an answer."

He shrugged. "Take the next exit. 71 South to 54 east to 13 south. That'll be the quickest route to Springfield."

I bit back a groan. "You know I grew up in the Ozarks. I've done some pretty extensive traveling between here and Springfield, so if you don't mind, I'll do my own navigating."

Dom chuckled. "Fair enough."

"Thank you."

"Did you get a chance to look through the files yet?"

"I was only given this assignment last night, but I did read through the first three murders." I wiggled my fingers while controlling the steering with my thumbs. They creaked with crepitus. I gave Dominic a cursory glance before turning on my left blinker and passing the eighteen-wheeler going sixty in a sixty-five. "He grabs his victims as they arrive home from work. He leaves no trace of himself behind, no DNA, fingerprints, hair, foreign fibers. There are no tire tracks leading to or from the abduction site. He's basically a ghost. He has spaced out his kills long enough that it took a while for the police to connect the cases. The first two victims were six months apart, and the third one eight months after that, then four months on this one. There doesn't seem to be a pattern to his killing. Within a week after the abduction, he places the body somewhere the family can find it. They always have a pinky toe missing, which the media has picked up on, and they are tortured with some kind of sharp implement." I could have recited the files word for word since I had an eidetic memory, but I found it creeped most people out when I put that ability on display. "Did I leave anything out?"

"This fourth case is the one you should have read."

I passed two more vehicles and settled back into the right lane of traffic. "Why's that?" I hadn't been given the fourth case to review.

Tartan held his phone screen up at an angle to show me a picture he'd pulled up on the screen. I was confused as I looked at a punch card with six paw prints punched out of twenty-eight tiny squares, and in the middle of the card was a bear logo with the words Blonde Bear Cafe Loyalty Card.

A wave of nausea washed over me.

"You know what this is, right?" Dom asked.

"Sure, it's a card from Blondina Messers' restaurant. I probably have one of those in my wallet. Once you buy twenty-eight meals, you get a free lunch or dinner. Are you telling me that was taken from the crime scene?"

"Don't have a heart attack, Agent Taylor. Your dad confirmed that the latest victim doesn't live in Peculiar. And appears to never have visited, either."

"The killer is a therianthrope?" Even though I was an FBI agent, I worked on the human side of the law. Suddenly it was perfectly clear why I'd been assigned to Dominic Tartan. This serial killer wasn't a human psychopath. Shit. We were looking for a shifter. "All the victims were shifters?"

"Yes." He looked at the tablet. "And this card proves the killer is familiar with your hometown."

I shook my head. "The killer can't be anyone from Peculiar. It's just not..." I shook my head again. "No."

"That card was found near the victim's front porch. It's got a gloss surface, so prints have been pulled, and they are running them through forensics," Dom said. "You wanted to know how we were partnered up? Well, Agent Taylor, I requested you."

"Because I'm from Peculiar?"

"Yes, that and it's an in. You know what these theri-anthrope towns are like. They are pretty closed up with integrators like me, and no human is going to be allowed to get in there to investigate. Your dad said we can work out of his office. We're going to check in with the locals in Springfield, get up to speed on the current victim, and then we are going to take our investigation to your hometown."

My knuckles were white again as I turned on to the 54-highway exit. "Great. Fun, fun." I guess I was going home.

Get it from your favorite eTailer!

ABOUT THE AUTHOR

I am a USA Today Bestselling author who writes paranormal mysteries and romances because I love all things whodunit, Otherworldly, and weird. Also, I wish my pittie, the adorable Kona Princess Warrior and my two cats Ash and Simon could talk. Or at least be more like Scooby-Doo and help me unmask villains at the haunted house up the street.

When I'm not writing about mystery-solving were-cougars or the adventures of a hapless psychic living among shapeshifters, I am preyed upon by stray kittens who end up living in my house because I can't say no to those sweet, furry faces. (Someone stop telling them where I live!)

I live in Mid-Missouri with my family and I spend my non-writing time doing really cool stuff...like watching TV and cleaning up dog poop

Follow Renee!
Bookbub
Renee's Rebel Readers FB Group
Newsletter